15

"I HAVE TO GO. I CAN'T STAY FOREVER, YOU KNOW."

"I know," Cassandra replied sadly. "You have to get back to your ranch."

"And you have to get back to Vegas," he added gently.

"That life means nothing to me," she answered impatiently. "You love me and I love you so why would you think I wouldn't come to Texas with you?"

"Because we'd be taking a hell of a chance. The hayseed and the hothouse flower! That's just too big a gamble."

"And you're the one who won't gamble—not even on something as important as our futures," she countered angrily.

"Especially our futures. Look, I'm trying to be reasonable," Jarratt replied heavily.

"Reasonable? You're just a coward who's willing to throw away everything because we might not make it."

"And you just want a free ride out of Vegas," Jarratt jeered.

"We both know that's not true," she said through clenched teeth. "I can find my own way out."

She looked at the clock on the wall. "Isn't your plane at six? I suggest you get on it and don't look back!"

A CANDLELIGHT ECSTASY ROMANCE ®

MIDNIGHT MEMORIES

Emily Elliott

A CANDLELIGHT ECSTASY ROMANCE ®

Published by
Dell Publishing Co., Inc.
1 Dag Hammarskjold Plaza
New York, New York 10017

Dell ® TM 681510, Dell Publishing Co., Inc.

Candlelight Ecstasy Romance®, 1,203,540, is a registered
trademark of Dell Publishing Co., Inc.,
New York, New York.

ISBN: 0–440–15614–9

Printed in the United States of America
First printing—December 1983

To Our Readers:

We have been delighted with your enthusiastic response to Candlelight Ecstasy Romances®, and we thank you for the interest you have shown in this exciting series.

In the upcoming months we will continue to present the distinctive sensuous love stories you have come to expect only from Ecstasy. We look forward to bringing you many more books from your favorite authors and also the very finest work from new authors of contemporary romantic fiction.

As always, we are striving to present the unique, absorbing love stories that you enjoy most—books that are more than ordinary romance.

Your suggestions and comments are always welcome. Please write to us at the address below.

Sincerely,

The Editors
Candlelight Romances
1 Dag Hammarskjold Plaza
New York, New York 10017

CHAPTER ONE

Just one more hour to go, Cassandra Howard thought gratefully as she slipped her tiny foot out of her sexy sandal and rubbed it surreptitiously against her other foot. She had been standing at her table on and off for the better part of seven hours, and her feet always began to feel the pinch about now. Slipping her foot back into the sandal, Cassandra shuffled her deck, stripped it down, and shuffled it again. Automatically she put a card at the bottom and began to deal.

Business has been slow tonight, she thought, even for a week night in September. The summer tourists had pretty well thinned out, and the patrons were for the most part wealthy businessmen and "high rollers," the serious gamblers who were the lifeblood of Las Vegas's casinos, which was why Cassandra could not figure out the man who had joined her game about a half-hour ago. He was standing in "first base," the position on the blackjack table just to the left of the dealer, where she could see him clearly. He was beautifully dressed in an expensive western-cut suit and had the customary thick wad of bills carried by the high rollers, but he was placing relatively small bets and losing most of those. Cassandra sneaked a look at him as the players finished their round. He was very tall, about her own age of thirty-three, maybe even a little younger.

7

Her mind on the stranger, Cassandra dealt the cards absently as she looked at the man.

Cassandra surveyed him curiously through lowered lashes. Crisp black hair was parted in the middle and combed back into two smooth wings. High cheekbones and dark eyes combined to give him a look that was perhaps a bit Mexican, although his tan was not any darker than that of any man who worked outdoors all day. And his well-muscled frame must have stretched at least a foot taller than her own five-foot three. Cassandra felt herself feeling very charmed by the broad grin the man bestowed on her every time she had to collect his money. In a town where handsome men were just as common as poker chips, this one had something more than just good looks. What was it? Cassandra wondered as she dealt another hand. Well, whatever it was, it wasn't his gambling ability. He had just lost again.

The man grinned as Cassandra collected his chips. She smiled back faintly, feeling a little sorry for him, and collected the chips from the rest of the players. Tonight she was working at a relatively high stakes table, a "quarter" table where the minimum wager was twenty-five dollars but the average bet was closer to five hundred with the occasional gambler betting upward of five thousand. The man in first base was only betting fifty dollars or so each round, and almost always losing that. But as she dealt a fresh round, she realized that from the looks of the outfit he had on he wouldn't miss his modest bets very much.

The good-looking man lost another round and paid up cheerfully. Really, why is he wasting his time in here? Cassandra asked herself. The players made their bets and played their cards, and Cassandra went back around the table collecting the chips yet again. This time the stranger won a hand, and as Cassandra counted out his winnings, he smiled charmingly and said, "Thank you, ma'am," in a soft Texas drawl. Cassandra's breath caught in her throat and she turned hurriedly to the next player. When the stranger smiled like that, he was devastating!

Cassandra dealt three more hands, but the man with the drawl did not win again. At exactly seven fifteen Cassandra's relief dealer came on to spell her for a fifteen-minute break and she escaped into the comfortable break room, where she gratefully sunk onto a sofa and kicked off her shoes. Larry, one of her fellow dealers, handed her a cup of lukewarm coffee and sank down on the sofa beside her. "Slow day," he commented idly.

"No kidding!" Cassandra agreed in her bubbling soprano. "There hasn't been one interesting thing happen all afternoon." Well, almost nothing, she amended to herself as she thought of the dark-haired stranger who had smiled at her so engagingly. She wondered again what he was doing in the casino, since he was clearly no expert at gambling.

"Well, just two more days and Margie and I take off for Europe for three weeks," Larry crowed. "Then we should see some excitement. How about you? When is your vacation?"

"Not until February," Cassandra replied, sipping her coffee and rubbing her sore feet on each other. "And I can hardly wait! Am I going to have a good time spending my money!"

"You going to Europe too?" Larry asked.

"Lord, no," Cassandra replied as she wrinkled her short, well-formed nose. "I'm going east for a few weeks."

"What's in the East?" Larry asked as he refilled his coffee cup. "Family?"

"No, they're in Minnesota," Cassandra replied. "I go east for the antiques."

"Ah, yes, our casino packrat," Larry teased as he reached out and ruffled Cassandra's uninhibited mop of

9

springy brown curls. "We've got to go back out there," he said cheerfully as he unceremoniously pulled her up by her arms. Retaliating, Cassandra waited until Larry had his back to her and jabbed her fingers into Larry's ribs, laughing when he came up six inches off the floor. Both were still laughing as they walked back into the pit, and even a stern look from Joe, the pit boss, failed to quell their good spirits.

The first thing Cassandra noticed when she got back to her table was that her good-looking stranger had left. She looked around the pit and glanced at the adjoining bar, but could not spot a tall head of raven hair. Chiding herself for being disappointed that he had gone, she shuffled her hand and dealt the first round. Quickly and methodically she played hand after hand, winning often enough so that her PC, or her percentage of profit, would be high, but never winning consistently enough to be assigned to a really high stakes table, where the minimum bets were always in the thousands. She wondered about the stranger as she played. Who was he? Where did he come from? And what had he been doing at her table?

The band in the bar was playing a popular disco tune, and a group of Japanese tourists were trying out all the latest steps when Joe approached Cassandra. "Have a request for you," he said noncommittally.

"Yeah, what is it?" Cassandra said as she dealt yet another hand.

"That guy that was sitting in first base wants you to have a drink with him," Joe said loudly, trying to talk over the band in the bar.

Cassandra expelled an exasperated breath, only hearing the second half of Joe's statement. "Joe, you know I'm not into that," she said tightly, a scowl on her usually cheerful face. Although the request was only for her company at the bar, Cassandra knew that it would inevitably lead to an invitation to his room, for a price, of course.

"What?" Joe said.

"I said I'm not into that!" Cassandra snapped loudly just as the band stopped playing suddenly. Both Cassandra and the dancers were caught unawares, the dancers moving for a moment or two in rhythm to a beat that no longer existed, and Cassandra shouting into a suddenly quieter casino. Several patrons turned to stare at her, and she blushed a fiery shade of red.

"Well, you don't have to be nasty about it," Joe said in a huff as he walked off. As he wandered toward his station in the middle of the pit, Cassandra caught a glimpse of a tall man with hair shining like a raven's wing standing patiently at the station. It had been the unlucky gambler! He had wanted her to go out with him! Thoroughly put out now and not sure why, Cassandra turned back to her game. It was not the first time she had been requested through the pit boss to go out with a man, and it wouldn't be the last. So why was it bothering her tonight?

Unfortunately the casual invitation that led to other things was as common in Las Vegas as blackjack and slot machines. Although there were women, plently of them, who did nothing but that for a living, a lot of the women dealers and barmaids were not averse to making a little, and sometimes a lot, of money on the side as part-timers. Intellectually Cassandra accepted the practice as part of the Las Vegas scene, but deep down it bothered her and made her feel very uneasy. Not only would she have been the last woman to indulge in that kind of thing, but she hated seeing other women degrading themselves in that manner. In spite of her revulsion, Cassandra had always refused the occasional request with good grace, but tonight she found herself annoyed by the entire procedure, in part because the stranger thought that she would do

11

something like that, and in part because he was very appealing to her and she would not have minded meeting him and getting to know him.

At exactly three minutes to eight pit security unlocked Cassandra's drop box, situated under the table where the day's earnings were placed, and replaced it for the swing shift that was coming on now and worked until four in the morning. Cassandra usually preferred working the swing to working noon to eight, but this month she had volunteered to fill an empty slot in the day shift, and so was coming off just as her usual crowd was coming on. There was much visiting and teasing as the shifts changed, and Cassandra was a little behind the other dealers as they walked back to the break room to either clock out and go home or get spruced up for a night on the town. Cassandra thought that she would probably do the former. Although it would have been easy enough to go with some of the other dealers to a buffet or a disco, the thought of several more hours on the Strip did not appeal to her tonight.

"Mind if I join you?" a deep voice drawled at her elbow, taking Cassandra by surprise. Startled, she whirled around and stared up, fascinated, into the eyes of her dark-haired stranger.

This close, he was more compelling than handsome. His face was really too angular to be considered truly good-looking, but the sensual curve of his lower lip hinted at a strongly sexual nature. He smiled at her easily, ignoring the admiring looks coming from two women in the pit and concentrating his charm on Cassandra. Oh, damn, why did he have to wait for her? she thought crossly. Now she would have to refuse him in person, and that was going to be hard to do. For the first time in her life she was tempted to go! Taking a deep breath, Cassandra looked up into his craggy face, hoping her eyes did not reflect her inner conflict. "I'm sorry," she said shortly. "I believe my

12

pit boss explained to you that I don't go in for that kind of thing."

"Yes, I heard you," he replied as he laughed softly. "As did most of the pit." He grinned wickedly as she blushed again. "I realize that you don't do that."

"Then why did you wait?" Cassandra asked curiously. "Why didn't you just ask for somebody else?"

"Because frankly I'm glad that you don't," he replied, throwing Cassandra off balance a little. "You seemed like a nice little person under that ridiculous bow tie and I wanted to get to know you this evening. Just get to know you. That's all." Cassandra fingered the bright red bow tie that was part of her Tropical Paradise uniform. "I thought that this being Las Vegas, I would have to pay for the privilege," he added candidly.

"Lord, no, you wouldn't have to pay to get to know me!" Cassandra laughed equally honestly, tingling with genuine pleasure at the stranger's outrageous flattery. "Thank you for the compliment," she said as she made a move toward the break room.

The man laid a gentle hand on her arm, not holding her arm in any way but letting his light touch stop her flight. Intrigued, Cassandra turned back to face him. "I meant it," he said softly. "I'd like to get to know you this evening."

"Well, I don't know," Cassandra stammered slowly, her grin fading a little. She usually did not go out with strangers, since that could be a little dangerous in a town like Las Vegas, where every sort of weirdo turned up sooner or later. Yet she really would have liked to spend the evening with this man, if only to find out more about him and maybe even learn what he had been doing at her table. Doubtfully she looked up at him. "Just what did you have in mind?" she asked softly.

"Nothing sinister," he said smoothly, accurately deducing the reason for her reluctance to go out with him. "Just dinner in a buffet and some good conversation. Look here," he said suddenly, whipping out his wallet and holding it out to her. Slowly she took the wallet and read his driver's license. Jarratt Vandenburg. From his birthdate she calculated that he was not quite thirty-two. His address was given as a route number out of Pecos, Texas. On the other side of his driver's license she spotted a Neiman-Marcus credit card and an American Express gold card. Nothing but the best for this one, she thought a bit cynically, then wondered again why he had been placing such small bets. "See?" he asked genially. "Now you know all about me, except whether or not I'm married, which I can assure you that I'm not. Now, how about it?" he asked with a challenging grin.

Cassandra tossed her curly head and smiled up at him. She was known for her warm, impulsive nature, and tonight she responded in character. Besides, any man naive enough to whip out his wallet in Las Vegas and hand it to a total stranger had to be harmless! "Sure, I'd just love to," she said eagerly, not noticing Jarratt's surprise at her delighted reply. "Let me chuck this uniform and I'll be right with you!" she said exuberantly, suddenly looking forward to the impromptu evening ahead.

Cassandra pulled a brush through her medium-length curly hair and stared at herself critically in the mirror. Not too bad, she thought as she wiped the mascara smudges out from under her eyes and splashed cold water on her face. Thanks to her youthful features and her curvaceous body, she did not look thirty-three. In her teens and twenties she had cursed the fates that had made her look younger than her years, but now she enjoyed her youthful appearance, feeling that it gave her a wider selection of potential friends and dates. Did Jarratt realize that she was a little older than he was? She shrugged her shoulders and applied a fresh coat of lipstick. It didn't much matter if he did realize it, or if he cared. She would probably never see him again after tonight anyway.

Cassandra dusted her face with a light coat of translucent powder and added a little color to her cheeks. She admitted to herself that her bouncing, vibrant looks, attractive and sexy rather than pretty, fit her personality, or at least used to fit her personality, like a glove. Lately she just hadn't felt like her old self and that bothered her. Quickly brushing away those thoughts before they had time to take hold, Cassandra stripped off the white blouse and the bow tie that was her Tropical Paradise uniform and replaced them with an apricot silk blouse and an ornate gold choker that she had found in an antique store. Her black pants were expensive and almost new, and her strappy black sandals, although not the most comfortable shoes she owned, were quite presentable. Cassandra turned sideways and sucked in her breath. Damn! That five pounds that she was constantly battling had reappeared and settled on her bottom, but thank goodness her stomach was still flat. Still, her figure, although fuller than she might have wished, was beautifully proportioned and just a little plump. She would do.

Jarratt was waiting for her as she left the break room. "What a transformation," he said lightly as he took her arm and escorted her through the casino. Cassandra had become accustomed to the opulent hotel and casino, but tonight she was seeing it through Jarratt's eyes, and she had to admit that, as always, the Tropical Paradise was impressive. The entire hotel was built around a Polynesian theme, and the decorators had done a marvelous job of recreating the atmosphere of a lush Pacific island, down to importing the native grasses and growing them in the casino and lobby of the hotel. But Cassandra found herself watching the people in the casino rather than looking at the trappings. As she and Jarratt strolled through the casino and lobby they spotted three families of Japanese tourists frantically competing at the roulette wheel, a Saudi with probably two hundred thousand dollars in a briefcase and two bodyguards on either side of him, and an elegant Indian and his wife with matching diamonds in their noses, who were just looking on, as well as the usual rich Americans and Mexicans with their rolls of bills. Jarratt looked around and shook his head. "Is it always like this?" he asked in wonder as he pushed open the heavy glass door for her.

"Summer is worse," Cassandra admitted as she took his arm and they walked out of the hotel into the desert air. "Then you get all the American tourists along with everybody else. Boy, what a crowd that makes!" As Cassandra and Jarratt walked down the steps, a well-known comic was stepping out of a limousine and walked up the steps into the hotel.

"Was that . . . ?" Jarratt asked.

"Sure was," Cassandra replied nonchalantly. "He's a regular here. He's played my table a few times. I like him a lot."

"I've always enjoyed his movies," Jarratt said as he led the way to the parking lot, where he unlocked the door of an obviously rented Ford. Cassandra slid in and Jarratt shut the door, then walked around the car and got in on the other side. Such nice manners, Cassandra thought as she watched him maneuver the car through the heavy traffic on the Strip. And he was so attractive! Cassandra was tempted to reach out and pinch Jarratt to see if the man was real.

Jarratt drove down the gaudy Strip for a few blocks and parked in front of a popular buffet and casino. He helped Cassandra out of the car and they went inside, walking past the rows of slot machines and taking their place in the long line. The lobby was noisy with the clanking of dishes, the blare of canned music coming over the PA system, and the ticking and ringing of slot machines, making conversation almost impossible. Jarratt and Cassandra waited in the long line in silence, postponing any talk until their plates had been piled high from the generous buffet and they had seated themselves in a relatively secluded corner of the dining room.

Jarratt looked up from his loaded plate and smiled. "Do you realize that I've managed to take you out, and that I don't even know your name?" he said as he sliced a thick slab of roast beef.

"I'm Cassandra Howard," she replied as she nibbled a bite of a delicious fruit salad. "My mother called me Cassie, but since she died I've been Cassandra."

"Have you always lived here?" Jarratt asked as he sipped his iced tea.

"No way!" Cassandra laughed as she ate a forkful of fried fish. "I grew up in Minnesota and moved to Vegas a few years ago. How about you? Are you on vacation?"

"Not exactly," Jarratt replied. "I'm on a buying trip. I need a few new bulls."

"Sounds more like a bunch of bull to me," Cassandra taunted saucily. She laughed at his indignant expression. "Now, don't you say a word!" she said as she brandished a fork in his face. "You know that you and every other rich Texas rancher spend thirty minutes on one of those cattle ranches and write off your entire vacation as a buying trip."

"I'll have you know that I bought four bulls this morning!" Jarratt replied with mock indignation. "This most certainly is a business trip!"

"And how long are you going to stay here?" Cassandra asked innocently.

17

"Two weeks," Jarratt replied sheepishly.

"Ah-ha!" she said. "See there? Your business took a half-day. You're writing this off!"

"Of course I am," Jarratt replied dryly. "I just bought ten thousand dollars worth of bull. I need to write something off."

Cassandra did some quick mental arithmetic. "Expensive little critters," she said wryly. In spite of the atmosphere that she worked in, ten thousand dollars for four animals sounded like a lot of money.

"Those are just for breeding commercial calves," Jarratt replied indifferently. "I've paid ten or fifteen thousand a head for an occasional show quality bull."

"Wow!" Cassandra said, impressed and not bothering to hide it. "That's a lot of money."

"You should talk," Jarratt scoffed as he sampled his apple pie. "You deal with several times that every working day, and I'll bet you've seen people drop that much on a single bet."

"More," Cassandra admitted as she sipped her hot coffee. "Although it used to awe me more than it does now. When I first got here I would gawk at these high rollers coming in with their suitcases of money and their bodyguards. Now I just stare a little and go on."

"How long have you been a dealer?" Jarratt asked as he proceeded to demolish his pie.

"Ten years," Cassandra replied without batting an eyelash. Jarratt looked at her in amazement and she laughed out loud. "If I can trust your driver's license, I have nearly two years on you."

"My God, you don't look it," Jarratt said honestly, and then colored to the roots of his hair when he realized what he had said.

"That's okay," Cassandra replied as she reached out and patted Jarratt's hand. "You know what Ben Franklin

18

said about older women. He recommended them because they are always so grateful!" She laughed out loud at his embarrassment, then took pity on him. "Tell me about your ranch," she said. "Is it large?"

"Seventy-five thousand acres or so," Jarratt admitted as Cassandra's eyes grew in amazement. "But that won't support near as many cattle as the same acreage would in the South or the Midwest."

"That's still big," Cassandra pointed out. She looked at him curiously. With that kind of land and considering the money that he had spent on his new bulls, Jarratt Vandenburg was obviously a wealthy man, yet he had placed very modest bets at her table. She wrinkled her nose and looked at him. Something just didn't add up. She knew that Jarratt was wondering why she was looking at him so strangely. Her curiosity getting the better of her, she finally blurted out, "Why did you make such small bets today?"

Jarratt laughed at her confusion, then lowered his voice conspiringly. "Can you keep my deepest secret?" he asked wickedly.

"S-sure," Cassandra stammered, totally confused.

Jarratt leaned over the table and placed his lips close to her ear. "I'm a lousy gambler," he whispered.

Cassandra laughed out loud. "I knew that!" she sputtered.

"No, really," Jarratt said, now speaking normally. "I really am a lousy gambler. I've never won, so I simply refuse to throw money away like that." His face sobered. "In fact, I'm just not a gambler, period. I never invest my money unless I know the deal is a sure thing. I've passed up a few deals that would have made me really rich, but then I haven't lost the family fortune like some people have either."

Cassandra looked at Jarratt in surprise. She would have

credited him with more daring than that. "Why are you so cautious?" she asked as delicately as she could.

"My dad was a gambler, and a loser," he admitted. "He gambled at everything—his money, his ranch, his love—everything. And he lost it all, except the ranch, and even then I just finished paying off his debts on it last year. I seem to have inherited his losing streak, so I don't gamble on anything that matters."

Cassandra nodded slowly. "Then what were you doing at my table?" she asked, puzzled. "Those stakes were pretty high for a non-gambler."

"I wanted to see you up close and meet you if I could," Jarratt admitted frankly. "I figured that was the only way to do it."

"I'm flattered," Cassandra said softly as she leaned back in her chair. And she was. In fact she was delighted that such an attractive man would care that much about meeting her, enough to play at her table and proposition her through Joe. Cassandra wasn't sure, but she would have bet a month's tips that Jarratt had never had any intention of taking her up to his room, even if she had agreed to go. He just did not seem like the kind of man who would have bought a woman's favors. He had simply wanted to meet her, just as she had wanted to meet him, and he had gone about it in the most direct way possible.

Jarratt asked her about her life as a dealer, and they sat and talked long after the busboy had cleared their plates. Cassandra told Jarratt how she had arrived in Las Vegas ten years ago with forty dollars to her name and persuaded the pit boss at a small, run-down casino on glitter gulch to hire her. She told him about the other two small casinos she had worked for and how she had worked at Caesars Palace for three years. She admitted that she felt extremely lucky to have landed a job at the Tropical Paradise when it opened a year ago. Prompted by Jarratt, she

20

told stories of all the celebrities that had played at her table over the years, and recounted for him her memories of some of the high rollers that she had played against and beaten or been beaten by. And at the same time Cassandra was thinking about the open, honest man across the table from her, a man who admitted that he was a lousy gambler and who made no apology for it. Just a few short years ago Cassandra would have found him hopelessly square, out of it, but tonight she looked at him with more mature eyes and definitely liked what she saw. Yes, he was physically appealing to her, even though they had only touched fleetingly. She wondered for a moment what it would be like to press her face against his hard chest and breathe his masculine scent, or to reach up and pull his head closer to her own, finally reaching those hard lips and locking them to hers. But it was not just Jarratt's physical appeal that had Cassandra so smitten. She actually found herself drawn to Jarratt's open, honest, genuine personality and wholesomeness, and she was amazed. Well, not too wholesome, Cassandra thought as she watched that sensuous lower lip curl around his coffee cup. Jarratt Vandenburg had probably had his share of moments, like any other virile male, but he was definitely different from the usual man that Cassandra had known in Las Vegas. She had not been around a man like Jarratt in a long time, and she frankly found him a delightful and refreshing change. Cassandra was surprised at herself. Then she glanced at Jarratt and shook her head inwardly. *Of course you're attracted to him,* she thought. *Any woman breathing would be.*

Cassandra set down her coffee cup and the busboy pointedly removed it. She and Jarratt glanced around and realized that the buffet was packed and that their table was sorely needed. Almost in unison they rose, and Jarratt left a tip on the table and took Cassandra's arm. His forearm

21

was hard and warm beneath the expensive cloth of his suit, and Cassandra held it a little tighter than she had to, feeling his hard muscles through his coat.

"I enjoyed dinner," Cassandra said as Jarratt stuffed his change into his wallet.

"You sound as though the evening is over," Jarratt chided softly. "Do you want to go home?"

"Oh, no!" Cassandra said eagerly. She most certainly did not want to go home yet!

"Then how about a little gambling?" Jarratt asked smoothly.

"I—I don't know," Cassandra said softly. "Maybe we could do something else—dance, maybe?"

"I would think that you'd like to gamble," Jarratt replied. "Or is there some rule that says you can't gamble in other casinos?"

"Oh, heavens, no, there's no rule like that," Cassandra laughed. "To them I'm just another customer. They're just as eager to get my money as they are to get yours."

"Then why are you hesitating?" Jarratt asked her arrogantly. "Don't you like to gamble?"

"Are you kidding?" Cassandra replied. "I love it! I even carry a few bills with me all the time, so if I get the urge I can indulge. But what about you? I don't want you to lose any more of your money."

"Sweet thing, I can afford it," Jarratt laughed. "Besides, I want to see what a pro can do."

Cassandra looked longingly into the casino. She would love nothing more than a few games of blackjack. She looked up at Jarratt and nodded, then reached out and grasped him by the wrist. "Come on!" she said brightly. "You're on!"

CHAPTER TWO

As Cassandra and Jarratt walked through the doors into the smoky casino, Cassandra could feel her blood start to quicken in anticipation of the coming competition. Although she was in no way a compulsive gambler, sometimes going for months without gambling for fun, she dearly loved the keen competition and the unexpected surprises that awaited her at the blackjack table. As she and Jarratt made their way to the cashier to pick up some chips, she reached into her purse and fumbled for her wallet. Suddenly, strong fingers circled her wrist and pulled her hand out of her purse. "I'll pay tonight," Jarratt said firmly.

"Don't be silly," Cassandra said, trying to extricate her hand from his grasp. Although Jarratt's touch was light, it was firm and she could not break his hold on her.

"I said I'll pay," Jarratt said again.

"No, you won't," Cassandra said impatiently. "I pay for my own gambling, thank you." She had never liked a man to pay for her chips.

The man at the window looked at them impatiently. "Next?" he said pointedly.

Jarratt pulled his wad of bills out of his pocket. "Two thousand dollars," he said calmly.

"That's too much!" Cassandra hissed at him. Jarratt and the man ignored her, and the man counted out two thousand dollars worth of chips in various colors. Jarratt quickly split the chips into two equal piles and handed one to Cassandra. "I don't need near that much," she protested as the next customer at the window elbowed her away.

"Why don't you just humor me?" Jarratt asked as they made their way to a quarter table much like the one that Cassandra had left just a few hours earlier. "Besides, I thought that I'd get us enough chips to last all night."

"Jarratt, these chips would last me a week!" Cassandra laughed as she finally figured out what was going on. Jarratt did not realize that on the playing side of the blackjack table Cassandra was a winner.

They took their places on the table. Cassandra was in "center," the spot directly across from the dealer, and Jarratt was between center and "third base," just to her left. Quickly the dealer shuffled, stripped, shuffled, put down a card, and dealt.

A good hand, Cassandra thought idly as she glanced at her cards. She thought that she would not ask for any more. She bet fifty dollars on her hand, in which she had cards worth eighteen points. Sure enough, the dealer was holding cards worth only seventeen. She collected her winnings, smiling encouragingly at Jarratt as he paid up his bet. She placed another bet, one hundred dollars this time, and asked for another card when she did not like the hand that she held. Sure enough, she won another round. Her hand was worth nineteen points, and the dealer's was worth only sixteen. The dealer pushed her the winning chips across the table, and Cassandra knew instinctively that it was going to be her game tonight.

Cassandra played cards the way she did everything else, impulsively and wholeheartedly, and she was surprisingly good at it. She had never learned to "count" or to use any other form of trickery, even in her job. She had acquired a certain amount of skill in the game, of course; that came with the territory, but she played completely honestly, depending on her instinct to guide her actions at the table. And usually that instinct guided her well, as it was tonight.

She won three more hands in a row, and raised her bets to two hundred dollars. Absorbed in her game, she barely noticed when Jarratt lost the last of his chips and bowed out, relinquishing his place to a middle-aged businessman. Cassandra was vaguely conscious of Jarratt standing at her elbow, watching every move she made. As the pile of chips in front of her became larger and larger, a small group of "lookers" stood around the table, watching Cassandra as she won hand after hand. She played again and again, studying each hand and making her decision quickly and calmly, the only outward sign of her mounting excitement a becoming flush on her cheeks.

Cassandra played for two hours, placing her bets with an outward calmness that she did not feel and watching her pile of chips grow as she played her luck against the house. Finally she decided to play one more round and call it a night. She watched the dealer shuffle and strip. Should she make her last bet a large one? Should she bet the entire stack of chips? What if she lost it all? She looked at Jarratt, feeling his dark eyes boring into her with an expression of grim astonishment. *He realizes what I'm going to do and he can't believe it,* she thought, remembering his cautious attitude. Somehow Jarratt's amazed expression only made Cassandra more determined to gamble it all. Slowly she pushed out the entire pile of chips.

She licked her lips as the dealer laid down the cards. Slowly she picked up her hand. *My God,* she thought, *a queen and an ace!* Blackjack! Breaking into a huge grin, she presented her cards and collected her winnings. As she began to gather up her chips, some of the lookers began to urge her to continue. "Come on, honey, you're on a winning streak!" an elderly lady with a rhinestone necklace cried.

"Hey, man, don't quit now!" a punk rocker with a Mohawk haircut said. Several others voiced their agreement.

"No, folks, I'm through," Cassandra demurred as Jarratt helped her gather up the last of her chips.

As she and Jarratt made their way to the cashier's window, Rocky Carlson, the manager of the casino, approached them with a wry expression. "Been cleaning me out again?" he asked Cassandra.

"Just a little," Cassandra said in an understatement.

"I just don't see how you do it," Rocky complained. "You must have a system."

Cassandra's temper flared before she could stop it. She hated to be accused of cheating, even in jest. "You know I don't count!" she snapped.

Rocky held out his palms ingratiatingly. "I know that," he said soothingly. "I'd vouch for your honesty anytime, Cass, you know that."

"Sorry, Rocky," Cassandra apologized. "I've forgotton my manners. Rocky, this is Jarratt Vandenburg from Texas. Jarratt, Rocky Carlson."

The two men shook hands and sized each other up. Undoubtedly Rocky probably wondered what hick town Jarratt came from, Cassandra thought cynically, and if he has hayseed in those expensive boots. And Jarratt had probably figured Rocky for what he was, too, a slick and charming operator who could sweet-talk himself into or out of almost anything, but who had about as much depth as a cheap mirror. Jarratt's hard body and proud posture spoke of hard work and a demanding but rewarding existence, but Rocky's artful slouch and indolent paunch spoke eloquently of too much self-indulgence. And to think that at one time she had thought that Rocky and all the others like him were the epitome of successful masculinity! She must have been out of her ever-loving mind!

Jarratt and Rocky made small talk for a few moments, then Jarratt took Cassandra's arm and he turned her toward the cashier's window. "Let's collect the loot before they change their minds," he teased as he nodded his head toward Rocky. "Nice to meet you," he said politely as Rocky grimaced a little. The cashier counted the chips and handed Cassandra five thousand dollars in cash. "Nice going," Jarratt said in awe as they walked away from the window.

Cassandra shrugged as she held out the hand with the money. "Maybe this will make up for what you lost this afternoon," she said.

Jarratt looked at the money and frowned. "Put that into your purse before somebody decides to relieve you of it," he said curtly.

"It's not my money," Cassandra protested as she held out her hand. "You bought the chips. It's yours."

"Don't be silly," Jarratt said firmly. "You won it."

"But I won it with your chips," Cassandra exclaimed. "I don't feel right taking it."

"That's the silliest thing I ever heard," Jarratt snorted as he led her toward the bar that was on the other side of the buffet. The buffet was still packed, even though it was twelve thirty in the morning. He led Cassandra to a relatively secluded corner table and sat her down, pushing firmly on her shoulders. He sat down in the chair across from her and she laid the pile of bills between them on the table. They stared at each other in exasperation for a moment, then Jarratt spoke. "Why do you want to give me the money back?" he demanded imperiously.

"I don't like to gamble with other people's money," Cassandra protested. "It makes me feel obligated, whether I really am or not. I wish you had let me buy my own chips. That way I could have kept it without worrying about it."

"You couldn't have afforded that much money," Jarratt said baldly.

"I wouldn't have needed that much," Cassandra shot back.

Jarratt stared at her determined face for a moment. "We'll compromise," he said finally. "You take half, I take half." Cassandra shook her head. "That's my last offer," Jarratt said firmly. "Either you take half of it or you take all of it."

Cassandra looked into Jarratt's face, reading from his expression that he was not going to change his mind. "All right," she said grudgingly as Jarratt split the money between them and put his half back into his wad of bills. Cassandra put her share into her purse. A tired-looking waitress appeared at their table. Jarratt ordered a Scotch on the rocks and Cassandra ordered a tequila sunrise.

"You surprise me," Jarratt said frankly as the waitress wandered toward the bar with their order, but not before she had examined Jarratt with appreciative thoroughness.

"How's that?" Cassandra asked.

"Most of the women I know would have been delighted to take that money," Jarratt replied.

"Well, I'm not most women," Cassandra replied. "I've never liked hustling and—"

"Just a damn minute!" Jarratt barked. "I thought we established back at the hotel that I wasn't interested in anything like that!"

"Hold on," Cassandra said placatingly, holding up her palms in a gesture of peace. "I meant nothing sexual. Here in Las Vegas the term *hustler* refers to anybody who makes money off the tourists in any way, shape, or form. It can be sexual or it can be providing companionship, an evening of flirting, almost anything."

"How does it work?" Jarratt asked curiously.

"Any number of ways, but chip hustling is the most common hustling you'll see out here. A girl wants to have a good time and make a little money too. So she spends the evening flirting and gambling with some guy who is convinced that she's bringing him luck and she drops money into her purse all night long. Now, I know that isn't what we were doing," she said quickly as Jarratt began to look angry again, "but I always feel that way if I gamble someone else's money."

"You're silly," Jarratt retorted as the waitress delivered their drinks. He smiled warmly and Cassandra felt herself wanting to kiss those smiling lips. "And surprisingly Victorian in spite of living here and being a dealer. Don't you realize that most of those men know exactly what's going to happen when they call those girls over?"

"I guess you're right," Cassandra conceded as she tasted her drink. She wrinkled her nose as the tasty concoction slid down her throat. "But I'll never forget the one and only time I did it. I felt crummy about it for a month! I'm afraid that I'm just too honest."

Jarratt looked at her shrewdly. "I certainly don't question that," he said slowly. "But how do you do so well at cards? You were something else out there, and you know it."

Cassandra looked at him resentfully, then realized that he was not doubting her honesty as so many had in the past. He was genuinely curious. "I'm lucky," she said simply. "I must have an instinct or something. I can just look at those cards and know whether to take another card or not. I don't have to count cards, to compute whether the other hands are high or low, the way professional gamblers do."

"And dealers?" Jarratt asked quietly.

"And most of the dealers," she acknowledged ruefully. "I'm a rare bird, I'll admit."

"But where on earth did you learn how to play?" Jarratt asked. "Luck or no, you had to learn it somewhere."

"From my father," Cassandra said. "He played poker nearly every week, sometimes more often in the winter when there wasn't much else to do, and he taught me as soon as I had learned math at school. By the time I was eleven, I was sitting in on his Friday night poker games and usually beating the socks off the rest of the men."

"But not your father?" Jarratt asked.

"Never Daddy," she admitted. "He could have made a fortune in this town."

"Why don't you?" Jarratt asked.

"Why don't I what?" Cassandra asked curiously.

"Why don't you make a fortune yourself?" Jarratt asked. "Just be a professional gambler?"

"You mean be a player?" Cassandra asked. "Oh, I'm not that good. I could lose my shirt."

"I wouldn't mind seeing you lose your shirt!" Jarratt teased as he drained his glass.

Cassandra laughed out loud, but inwardly she felt a small tingle of excitement as she imagined Jarratt's strong fingers slowly unbuttoning the shimmering apricot blouse. "Look, it's late even for this crazy town," Jarratt said as he consulted his watch. "I'll take you back to your car so you can go home and sleep. Are you working tomorrow?"

Cassandra nodded wordlessly as she rose from her chair. Together they walked to his rented Ford, and Jarratt held the door for Cassandra and shut it firmly behind her. The Rocky Carlsons of this world could take some lessons in manners from this one, Cassandra thought as they drove back to the Tropical Paradise. But then the Rockys of this world could learn a lot of other things from a man like Jarratt. Not allowing herself to pursue that thought any further, Cassandra forced herself to concentrate on the bright blinking lights on the Strip. Even at two in the morning the lights were just as bright as they had been earlier in the evening, and Cassandra remembered that on her usual schedule she would still be at work. She smiled as she realized that on his ranch Jarratt would have been asleep for hours by now.

Jarratt pulled into the driveway of the Tropical Paradise and looked at her inquiringly. "Where's your car?" he asked softly.

"Around back," Cassandra replied, pointing out a narrower driveway coming off the main one. Jarratt swerved onto the smaller driveway and followed it around the mammoth hotel, finding the huge employee lot beyond the swimming pools and the outermost tennis court. The lot was certainly well enough lighted, although it seemed dim after the gaudy brightness of the Strip. "My car's on the third row almost all the way down," she said softly. "It's a red Firebird."

Jarratt drove slowly down the row until he spotted her car. He stopped in front of it and killed the engine, but he made no move to get out of the car, and neither did Cassandra. She watched him expectantly, wondering if he had been feeling the same sensual attraction for her that she had for him. She wondered if he would let her go without a kiss, or would he claim her lips as payment due? Cassandra ran her tongue around her lips in an unconsciously sensual gesture. When Jarratt made no move toward her, she turned to open the car door.

"Cassandra," Jarratt said softly. She halted her movement, one hand on the door handle. "Turn around so that I can kiss you good night."

Slowly Cassandra turned toward him, anticipation drumming the blood in her ears. Jarratt reached out and hooked one finger under her chin carefully so that his fingernail did not scratch her tender skin, and gently but firmly he pulled her face toward his. When she was close enough to smell his tangy aftershave and his musky skin, he held her face framed in his hands and lowered his mouth to hers, capturing her lips with his. His kiss began softly, exploring her lips lightly with his, and then as Cassandra moved unconsciously toward him, he groaned and gathered her into his arms, crushing her to him as he opened her mouth with his and explored its sweetness thoroughly. Cassandra moaned and arched her back to get closer to his masculine warmth. She was no novice to the act of kissing, but this storm of passion was taking her by surprise. It was only supposed to be a simple kiss! She curled her fingers into the smooth fabric of his coat and gloried in the feel of the taut muscles in his upper arms.

As far as Cassandra was concerned, the embrace and exploration could have lasted forever, but they did not. As slowly as they had come together, they finally eased apart. Jarratt pulled away from his crushing kiss and tasted her lips gently, then eased his head back from Cassandra's. She slowly unwound her fingers from his arms and sat up straight. It was as though each of them knew that one false move and they would be back in each other's arms, and neither of them was ready to face the consequences of that. Jarratt got out of the car and opened Cassandra's door, but he did not touch her again.

She unlocked the door of her car and turned to him. "Thank you for a lovely evening," she said in a voice husky with passion.

"My pleasure," Jarratt replied in an unsteady rumble. The wind ruffled the dark wings of hair, and his dark eyes captured hers.

Cassandra climbed into her car and drove away, leaving Jarratt standing in the middle of the parking lot with a bemused expression on his rugged face.

* * *

Cassandra sighed as she bent over the meat counter and selected a large, juicy steak and two smaller roasts. Meat was going up by the week! Oh, well, she could afford it. Her salary plus tips came to a very comfortable life-style, she had to admit, for a woman with a high-school education and no real skills to speak of.

Cassandra headed for the produce section absentmindedly, almost colliding with another cart laden with a week's worth of groceries for a hungry family. Even though it was three in the morning, the grocery store was packed with shoppers. Las Vegas was a twenty-four-hour town, and it had seemed at first to Cassandra that no one ever slept here. The Strip was alive twenty-four hours a day, and many of the other businesses in Las Vegas followed suit. Cassandra had decided on impulse to pick up a few items on her way home from her date with Jarratt, since she was not sleepy and she knew that she would just lay awake staring at the ceiling if she did go home.

Jarratt Vandenburg. Was he real? Cassandra wondered as she picked through a bin of tired-looking lettuce. Finding a head that was a little better than the rest, Cassandra tossed it into the cart and trudged toward the dairy section. He certainly seemed to be genuine, she thought, not at all like so many of the men in Las Vegas, residents and tourists alike. Jarratt had depth, Cassandra thought as she selected a quart of milk and two cartons of yogurt. He was open and direct, and there was more to him than met the eye. And don't forget that kiss, she added to herself as she picked up a package of cheese. Although Cassandra had been kissed many times in her life, never had a simple kiss set her on fire like Jarratt's had. Although Jarratt had known what he was doing, she could not credit his appeal and her response to mere expertise. Between them they had experienced an honest explosion of emotion that Cas-

33

sandra had not been expecting. Indeed, she had not even dreamed it possible.

Cassandra paid for her groceries, then drove to her condominium in the early morning darkness. She placed the perishables in the refrigerator and, suddenly tired, left the rest in the bags and padded wearily to her bedroom. Stripping off her clothes, she took a short hot shower and crawled naked into her cherrywood fourposter. She stared up at the canopy for a few minutes, reliving the feel of Jarratt's mouth on hers, then shrugged her shoulders and turned over. She would probably never see him again. Unreasonably disappointed by the thought, she turned over and shut her eyes.

The sound of the doorbell made its way into Cassandra's consciousness and, groaning, she turned over and stared at the clock. It was nearly eight already. *Oh, well,* Cassandra thought, *I've survived on a lot less sleep than this.* She pulled on a maroon silk kimono that she had picked up at a tourist trap on the Strip and wrapped the belt tightly around her, in case her caller was Mr. Hilliard, the retired banker across the drive. Peering out her peephole, she could see a distorted view of shimmering blond hair and perfect facial features staring patiently at the door. Smiling, Cassandra opened the door and took the hot coffeepot from her guest. "Come on in, Sharon, it's been too long."

As Sharon Burns stepped over the threshold, Cassandra wondered for the hundredth time how one young girl could be put together so perfectly. Sharon was the epitome of feminine perfection, from her flawless face to her long legs and perfectly manicured toes. But Sharon's eyes looked tired today, and she seemed a little thinner than usual. She smiled at Cassandra and produced a paper bag that she had been hiding behind her back. "I brought hot doughnuts, if you think your diet can stand them."

34

They both laughed, knowing that diet or no Cassandra could not resist the hot doughnuts. Cassandra led the way to her small patio off the kitchen and placed the coffeepot on the elegant glass table. Sharon, completely at home in Cassandra's apartment, gathered up plates and found the sugar bowl in the cabinet and followed Cassandra. Finally noting Cassandra's deshabille, she grinned sheepishly. "I bet I woke you," she said ruefully. "I thought you were working the day shift."

"I am," Cassandra yawned as she poured herself a cup of coffee and sniffed the air. The cool early morning air, dry and crisp, smelled of sand and desert, a peculiarly pleasant sensation. "I had a date last night."

"Somebody I know?" Sharon asked as she bit into a doughnut.

"No, a rancher from Texas took me out after my shift," Cassandra said as she took yet another bite.

"Rich, of course," Sharon said cynically. "Like all the rest."

"Now, Sharon," Cassandra chided, "he was very nice."

"Aren't they all?" Sharon said as she licked her fingers and reached for another doughnut. "Most of my dates are really pretty nice, too, I guess."

Cassandra eyed her young friend warily. Lately Sharon had been dating a string of middle-aged wealthy rogues who were old enough to be her father. Although she had not worked on a showline for several months, she always had money to spare and lately had sported several new and expensive pieces of jewelry. *Is Sharon doing what I think she's doing?* Cassandra asked herself as Sharon poured them both a fresh cup of coffee. Sharon had arrived in Las Vegas two years ago, fresh out of high school, to work as a showgirl, and she and Cassandra had met in a buffet line on the Strip. In spite of the difference in the women's ages, they had become fast friends and just last

35

month Sharon had rented the condominium at the end of the block. But since she had moved in, she had not worked in a single show, but spent all her time dating. *It's the life-style here,* Cassandra thought. *It's lured her in, and she doesn't even realize what it's done to her.* Oh, it wasn't just the men that Sharon was seeing. It was the drinking, the drugs, going days without adequate sleep, never thinking about tomorrow or taking into account that there might be consequences for what she was doing. Cassandra wrinkled her nose in thought and spoke cautiously. "What are these men you're seeing really like?" she asked.

"They're interesting," Sharon replied as her eyes became guarded. "And they treat me well. Very well." Sharon did not look Cassandra in the eye as she helped herself to another doughnut.

"But doesn't it ever get to you?" Cassandra asked as she looked at Sharon shrewdly. "I mean, going out all the time, the booze . . ."

Sharon shook her head. "Of course not," she said firmly, only the momentary uncertainty in her eyes indicating that it really did. "Have you seen the new disco around the corner from your hotel?" she asked brightly.

Cassandra let Sharon change the subject, but she studied her friend as they ate the rest of the doughnuts. Sharon was bright and cheerful, too much so for the mood to be genuine. *It's finally getting to her,* Cassandra thought. *Damn! Las Vegas has done a number on her. But what can I say?* Cassandra asked herself. It was one thing to think that your best friend had become a call girl, quite another to come out and say so.

They finished their breakfast and Sharon left, explaining that she had a ten o'clock date, and Cassandra finished the last cup of coffee in the pot and wandered into the bathroom for another shower, this one cool and invigorating. She soaped her body and washed her curly hair with a fragrant shampoo, thankful once again for her youthful face and vowing to lick those extra five pounds if it killed her, even though she admitted that her figure wasn't really all that bad. As she stood naked at her bathroom mirror combing her curly brown hair into place, she thought about Sharon and wondered if her earlier concern had been necessary. Was the life-style really all that bad for Sharon, or was she just projecting her own sour feelings into concern for the young woman?

Cassandra wandered into the bedroom and pulled on her lacy underwear. It was still too early to put on her uniform, so she pulled the maroon robe back on and curled up in the huge wing chair beside her bed. For once she did not push her unwelcome thoughts away as she had for the past months, but she allowed herself to take them out and examine them thoroughly.

Cassandra's lips curled into a slight smile as she remembered how a naive Minnesota girl thought she was going to take Las Vegas by storm. She had been very young and pretty and had innocently thought that the show directors would be able to use her modest talents as a dancer in one of their chorus lines. After several days she realized that her plans had been ridiculous in the extreme, but she had fallen in love with the glamor and the bustle of the gambling center and desperately wanted to stay. So she looked around for any kind of work that she could find, and was astonished to discover that her skill at poker was very salable. She quickly mastered the rules of blackjack and found a job at a small casino. She had perfected her talents as a dealer and at the same time had reveled in the excitement of her adopted home. She had never lacked for dates or for something to do. If she was bored, which was seldom, she called a friend or two and they went to a show, or chartered a boat for the day on Lake Mead, or rode dirt-bikes on the desert sand. And as she was able to get

37

jobs in the better casinos, her income improved and she was able to buy her own condominium and furnish it for the most part with antiques, and indulge in her love of expensive clothes and in an occasional good piece of jewelry. So why was she dissatisfied?

Cassandra frowned at her reflection in the ornate mirror over her dresser. Her hair was almost dry, so she picked up her brush and pulled it through the damp tangles, brushing her hair into a taffy-colored mane that framed her face. Cassandra peered at herself in the mirror. She honestly didn't look much different than she had when she came to Las Vegas, but she had definitely changed in ways that didn't show. *The life-style and pace are wearing thin,* she told herself, *only you don't want to admit it. You're as worn out as a glitter-gulch poker chip. You don't want to admit that you're tired of all the fun and the empty pleasure, that last night was the first date you've had in months because you're tired of the men around here.* Cassandra winced as she thought of how full and rich her mother's life had been at thirty-three and compared it to the shallowness of her own life of fun, of pleasure, of making and spending money. She had accomplished very little in her thirty-three years that meant anything at all.

But what on earth can I do about it? Cassandra wondered as she pulled on a pair of black slacks that were part of her uniform. It was one thing to decide that her life was meaningless, but quite another to give up a secure, well-paying job and go searching for rainbows. *And I don't even know what kind of change I want,* Cassandra thought as she slipped into her uniform shirt and tied her bow tie. She had been restless and unhappy for months, and she was no closer to a solution than she had been when the dissatisfaction had begun to plague her. As she skillfully made up her face, Cassandra thought of Jarratt. Had he been the reason for her sudden honesty with herself? Had her brief

38

acquaintance with the compelling Texas cowboy been the catalyst that had sharpened her own unhappiness with her life?

Would she ever see him again? Cassandra wondered as she picked up her purse and keys and headed for the door. Probably not, she thought. He had said nothing about taking her out again, and he did not have her address or telephone number. Still, she turned back and went into her bedroom, although it was time for her to go, and grabbed a silky green blouse out of the closet to take with her just in case. She could hope, couldn't she?

CHAPTER THREE

Cassandra glanced at the tiny wristwatch on her arm as she dealt another hand. It was nearly eight, and pit security should be around in a minute for the drop box. She sighed as she collected the winnings from the people on her table. Despite her feeling that morning that she would not see Jarratt Vandenburg again, unconsciously she had searched the room all day for a glimpse of those raven wings of hair towering above the crowd. She dealt another hand and chided herself for being silly. They had shared a casual date and a friendly good-night kiss. That was all. And if she had been foolish enough to read anything else into it, then it was her fault for being disappointed.

Just at eight pit security unlocked her drop box and put in another one. Cassandra turned the table over to the dealer on the swing shift and trudged toward the break room. Although she was tired from lack of sleep and working all day, she did not want to go home. Suddenly her comfortable apartment seemed unappealing. Yet she did not want to go out on the Strip with one of the other dealers either. Cassandra grabbed up her purse and headed for the back door. Maybe she could just drive around town for a while and see if she felt more like going home in an hour or so. No, she couldn't do that. The Firebird was being serviced. Damn, why had she expected the big

40

cowboy to come back around? He probably kissed everybody like that!

Cross, Cassandra pushed open the door to the break
room and marched through, promptly colliding with a
six-foot-plus wall of muscle and bone. She bounced off and
looked up, startled, into Jarratt Vandenburg's amused
eyes. Cassandra's eyes revealed her surprise and she
opened her mouth to speak, but nothing came out. It was
Jarratt!

"Were you in a hurry?" Jarratt asked easily.

Cassandra shook her head. "I—I was just going home,"
she stammered, still unable to believe it was Jarratt. He
had really come back!

"So early?" Jarratt teased. "I thought you might be
hungry again."

"Sure, I'm hungry," Cassandra said quickly. Jarratt
extended his arm and she took it, then withdrew her hand
quickly. "I look a mess!" she said as she ran back toward
the break room. "Let me change!" She hurried into the
break room with the sound of Jarratt's laughter ringing in
her ears.

Once in the ladies' room she tore off her uniform blouse
and pulled on the green one in record time, then freshened
her makeup and threw a white shawl around her shoulders.

Jarratt was waiting patiently for Cassandra, idly watching a hot game going on in the pit. The dealer was matching his wits with one of the best players in Las Vegas, and
was losing miserably. Cassandra slipped up to Jarratt and
slid her hand into his, and together they watched the game
in progress. Slowly the player won a larger and larger
share of the chips, until the dealer had to call for more
money. Jarratt was completely absorbed but Cassandra, in
spite of her interest in the gambling, was conscious of the
hard, warm, calloused palm that was holding her own tiny

41

hand so firmly. She remembered how those palms had felt as they carefully held her face steady for his kiss, and she shivered a little. The dealer was brought more chips and play resumed. They watched a few more minutes, then Jarratt squeezed her hand gently and led her away. "I get the feeling that game is going to go on all night," he said as he steered her toward the door.

"Probably," Cassandra agreed as they walked down the driveway to the parking lot. "What did you do today?" she asked with studied casualness.

"Slept for most of the morning," Jarratt admitted.

Cassandra stared at him, aghast. "Nobody sleeps in Las Vegas!" she protested.

"I do," Jarratt drawled. "Especially if I've been up for most of the past three nights. Those ranchers know how to entertain their customers!"

"So I've heard," Cassandra said dryly, remembering all the wild stories she had heard about the entertainment provided by the ranchers.

"And then I spent most of the afternoon wandering through all the hotels gawking," Jarratt admitted cheerfully. "I got stuck in a line for tickets to Wayne Newton tomorrow, or I wouldn't have been late picking you up. I was afraid I'd missed you."

"I thought you weren't coming," Cassandra said softly, her voice revealing some of the disappointment she had felt when she thought he would not return.

Jarratt stopped in his tracks and turned her to face him. "How could you think a thing like that?" he demanded softly. "After that kiss last night . . . ?"

Cassandra stood on tiptoe and planted a kiss on his jaw. "I had hoped you'd come," she said honestly.

"That's more like it," Jarratt said, smiling. He reached down and kissed the tip of her short nose, then ushered her to the Ford. "I want the name of your favorite restaurant in town," he demanded as he opened the door of the car. "Let's splurge tonight."

"All right," Cassandra replied as she cocked her head to one side and thought a minute. "I know a nice one that has a terrific view of the Strip. It's right down the street."

Cassandra gave Jarratt directions and he drove to one of the major hotels and parked, then they walked into the sumptuous lobby, this one decorated in a plush Victorian motif, and took the elevator to the restaurant on the top floor. Jarratt slipped the headwaiter a bill and soon they were seated at a table next to the window, where they could look out and see the Strip, running from downtown Las Vegas out into the desert. Jarratt ordered drinks while Cassandra surveyed her menu. The waiter took their order —chicken Kiev for Cassandra and prime roast for Jarratt. Then they sipped their drinks and stared out the window at the gaudy Strip.

"Romantic, isn't it?" Jarratt asked dryly.

"Oh, yes," Cassandra gushed, grinning. "You, me, and a couple million light bulbs! Seriously, it is beautiful, I guess, especially if a person has never seen it before."

"But not romantic?" Jarratt teased.

"No way!" Cassandra said firmly. "I would hardly call the Strip romantic."

"What would you call romantic then?" Jarratt asked, suddenly serious.

Cassandra bit back a flippant reply and thought a minute. Jarratt was serious, and she wanted to consider her answer carefully, although she was not sure why. "Moonlight, a blanket of stars maybe," she said slowly. "No one else for miles and miles. Quiet. A man I love." Cassandra stared into Jarratt's eyes, wondering what had made her add the last condition to her list.

Jarratt smiled gently. "It sounds very nice," he said softly.

43

The waiter arrived with their dinner, destroying the fragile mood. Cassandra did not know whether she was sorry or glad. She had felt uncomfortable with her admission, although she thought Jarratt might have added a few romantic thoughts of his own if they had not been interrupted.

Dinner was excellent, and Jarratt and Cassandra ate slowly, savoring every bite. They talked of Jarratt's ranch mostly, and Cassandra got a pretty good picture of the isolated, lonely life he led out there, with the nearest town forty miles away. Jarratt told her about Martha and Pete, the cook and foreman, who had been at the ranch since before he was born, and about the resident cowboys who lived in house trailers not far from the main house. He told her about the card games the cowhands played religiously, and about the weekly Saturday night drive into Pecos to sample the wild nightlife at the small local saloon. Cassandra listened, fascinated, to his narrative. Amazingly his life sounded wonderful to her. The hard work, the purpose, the ordinary people who kept the ranch going—they sounded fabulous. She wondered suddenly if Jarratt had any family. During a break in the conversation she asked quietly, "I gather from what you said last night that your father is dead. Do you have any other family?"

Jarratt's eyes clouded for a moment. "My mother's still alive," he said sadly.

"Is she all right?" Cassandra asked with a worried frown. Jarratt's sudden change of mood worried her.

"Mamacita's fine," Jarratt assured her, his face clearing. "She lives in El Paso with my stepfather and stepsister."

"What did you call her?" Cassandra asked in puzzlement.

"Mamacita," Jarratt said. "I've always called her that. My mother is Mexican-American," he explained.

44

"I didn't think you looked German," Cassandra said dryly. It occurred to her that Jarratt's unhappiness at the mention of his mother was still unexplained, but his good humor was restored, and Cassandra hesitated to ask him anything that would bring back his displeasure.

Cassandra refused dessert in deference to her waistline, but she sat patiently while Jarratt waded through a delicious-looking baked Alaska. As they sipped their coffee and stared out the enormous windows, Jarratt asked her if she liked to dance. At Cassandra's exuberant yes, he asked if she could suggest a good spot where they could do some "real dancing."

"Sure," Cassandra replied, thinking of all the intricate disco steps she loved to execute. "How about Paul Anka's Jubilation?"

"You're on!" Jarratt exclaimed as he signaled the waiter for the bill.

Jubilation was just about a half-block from the restaurant, so Jarratt and Cassandra elected to walk rather than drive the short distance. They were met by the formally dressed doorman and ushered through the interior garden and past the restaurant into the huge, auditoriumlike interior of the disco itself. It had one wall covered with speakers and the elevated dance floor was surrounded with mirrors and pulsed with the beat of the sound system. Cassandra could feel her body begin to throb to the rhythm of the music. "Come on, let's dance!" she said as she eagerly led Jarratt toward the dance floor.

Jarratt looked baffled for a moment, then took her arm and led her in the opposite direction. Equally confused, Cassandra followed him, although she desperately wanted to dance. He pulled her out of the disco into the interior garden and looked down into her face with a frown. "I thought you said we could dance here!" he exclaimed.

"Why, we can!" Cassandra shouted back over the noise.

"That's why I brought you here. This is the hottest disco in Vegas."

"Disco," Jarratt said flatly. He looked a little uncomfortable. "You want to disco?"

"And you want to dance all slow and cuddled up," Cassandra said slowly as she figured out what she had done. "Oops. I guess I goofed. I thought when you said you wanted to really dance—"

"That I really wanted to dance," Jarratt finished for her. "Frankly I've never even seen most of those steps out there." He looked back into the disco at the dancers on the dance floor. "Needless to say, we don't get much chance to do that kind of dancing in Pecos."

"How about Dallas or Houston?" Cassandra asked, feeling worse by the minute. She certainly had not meant to embarrass Jarratt!

"There aren't many discos left in Dallas," Jarratt admitted. "They've all gone urban cowboy."

Cassandra brightened. "Can you do those fast Western dances?" she asked eagerly.

"Of course," Jarratt scoffed. "I was weaned on those."

"Well, if you're coordinated enough to do those toe-twisters, you can do some disco," she said firmly. "Now, watch me for a minute and then step into place in front of me." Then unselfconsciously she launched into one of the less intricate disco patterns, moving her body smoothly and sensuously in time with the music. Jarratt watched, fascinated by the motion of her body, until Cassandra motioned him to her. Almost effortlessly he moved into place and was able to pick up the steps quickly.

"Now, here's another one," Cassandra said as she slipped into a more complicated pattern. Jarratt stumbled once but picked up the steps quickly. He whirled her around effortlessly, almost knocking the both of them into a waiter on his way to the kitchen.

"Sorry," Cassandra said unrepentantly to the exasperated waiter. "Well, that should hold us for the evening. Are you ready to make your debut?"

"As ready as I'll ever be," Jarratt replied as he took her arm and they walked back into the disco. The DJ was playing a Donna Summer hit, and Jarratt swung Cassandra out on the floor with all the self-confidence of a man who had been dancing disco for years, not minutes. And he danced well, surprisingly graceful for such a large man. He kept up with Cassandra through the swinging numbers, occasionally improvising a few steps of his own, and held her tight during the few slow numbers that the DJ played. Cassandra breathed in the tangy masculine scent radiating through the soft silk shirt that he wore and pressed her face into his chest. She could stay in his arms like this forever! Suddenly alarmed by her thoughts, she lifted her head and tried to pull away, but Jarratt's strong hand pushed her head back to his chest.

The DJ played a big-band tune, and they found an empty table in the corner of the room. Jarratt ordered his usual Scotch and Cassandra a tequila sunrise and they looked over the crowd. The dancers were dressed in elegant dancing costumes and many of the men had on tuxedos, but Cassandra was not out of place in her pants and fancy blouse, and Jarratt looked wonderful in his shining silk shirt and slacks. She noticed that his expensive boots had been replaced with an equally fine pair of dress shoes. As the DJ walked by their table Jarratt slipped him a few bills and whispered something into his ear. The DJ broke into a broad grin and nodded, then pocketed his money and headed back toward his booth.

"What did you ask him for?" Cassandra asked as she finished the last of her drink.

"Oh, nothing he couldn't handle," Jarratt grinned. Just then Johnny Lee's "Looking for Love" came blaring out of the speakers, accompanied by the DJ's gravelly voice-over.

"This is for all you Texans out there who are dying to do the two-step!" he called. A number of enthusiastic whoops could be heard from the various Texans in the crowd, and an enthusiastic run for the dance floor began.

"Come on, Cassandra," Jarratt laughed as he jumped up from his chair and pulled her toward the dance floor.

"But Jarratt, I can't two-step!" Cassandra protested.

"If you're coordinated enough to do all those fancy disco numbers, you can do the two-step," Jarratt parroted firmly as he led her up onto the dance floor and took her into his arms.

Cassandra had to admit that the dance was easy. It was more of an organized shuffle than anything else, yet Jarratt led her through the steps gracefully, holding her body close to his and splaying his fingers firmly around her waist. He must have tipped the DJ well, because the man played four western numbers in a row, leaving Jarratt and Cassandra and all the other Texans in the crowd breathless at the end. Laughing in sheer pleasure, they left the dance floor and Jarratt steered Cassandra toward the door. "It's late," he said as he bid the doorman good night.

"My God, it's after two!" Cassandra exclaimed as she consulted her watch. "Where has the time gone?"

"How does that go about having a good time?" Jarratt asked lightly. "Should I take you back to your car?"

"The Firebird's being serviced," Cassandra explained. "Would you mind taking me on home?"

"My pleasure," Jarratt said softly.

She gave him directions, and they drove to her condominium in silence. Cassandra's mind was working overtime. Did Jarratt expect to be invited to go inside with her? Should she invite Jarratt to come in? Cassandra would normally have not even considered inviting a man that she had just met to stay the night, but Jarratt was different. She wanted to invite him in, but she was afraid. Not of Jarratt, but of herself.

Jarratt parked in front of her front door and got out before Cassandra could speak. He opened her door and she climbed out slowly, the indecision in her mind clearly written all over her expressive face. Jarratt smiled faintly, then slammed her car door shut and picked her up and sat her on the hood of the car, only a little warm from the short drive from the Strip. "I can reach you better like this," he murmured as he bent his head slightly and captured her lips with his own.

Last night he had taken his time kissing her; tonight he plundered her mouth suddenly, opening her willing lips with his and savoring her sweetness. Cassandra melted into him, forgetting that she was on the street in front of her home, and that a streetlight was spotlighting the two of them. She arched her body toward his and reached around his lean waist, feeling the hard muscles in his back knot from the eager exploration of her tormenting fingers. Jarratt drew away from her mouth and trailed a path of kisses down her face and throat, leaving a moist quivering trail that felt a little cool in the night air. He then reached up with his hand and lightly palmed one breast, groaning when he felt her nipple stiffen through the silky fabric. Cassandra moaned as his fingers found her other breast and tickled it into awareness, becoming hard and firm against her lacy bra. Squirming with the pleasure he was bringing to her, she reached up with her lips and trailed a sweet row of kisses across Jarratt's stubbly jaw, wincing a little from the unexpected pain of his rough beard. Jarratt leaned down and kissed her tingling mouth, burning from the scraping of his beard.

"Sorry," he whispered. "You didn't need a mouthful of bristles."

"That's all right," Cassandra whispered, reaching up to caress his prickly jaw with her hand. She knew at that moment that if Jarratt asked to come in, she would have to say yes. She did not have it in her power to deny him. What he wanted, she wanted, even if it was not the best thing for her in the long run.

Jarratt pulled back from their heated embrace. "I'm leaving now while I still can," he whispered hoarsely. Cassandra nodded without speaking, relieved and yet at the same time disappointed. "I want you," Jarratt continued, "and you want me. I know that. But I don't think either of us is ready for that yet." Cassandra nodded again faintly, warmed by Jarratt's leashed desire. She was amazed by his sensitivity. He felt exactly the same way that she did about making love.

Jarratt ran his hand around the back of his neck. "Shall I pick you up tomorrow evening at the casino?" he asked as she fished in her purse for her keys.

"I'm off tomorrow," she remembered suddenly.

"Super!" Jarratt said, his voice slowly returning to normal. "Will you do the tourist rounds with me?"

I'd go to a dogfight with you if that's what you wanted to do, Cassandra thought. Out loud, she said, "Sure! Pick me up about eleven. Is that all right?"

Jarratt nodded. "See you then." He leaned forward and placed a hard kiss on her mouth, then turned and walked away without a backward glance. Cassandra could have sworn she heard him whistling "Looking for Love" as he hopped into the car.

Cassandra was waiting for Jarratt when he rang her doorbell promptly at eleven. She had been ready for the last thirty minutes, and had alternated between pacing the floor and repeatedly checking her makeup and hair. She was not really nervous. It was more like the anticipation that she had felt early on Christmas morning when she had come down the stairs and had spotted the gifts waiting for her under the tree. *Oh, boy,* she thought, *wouldn't Jarratt make some lucky woman a wonderful Christmas present!*

"Mornin'," Jarratt said softly as Cassandra pulled open the door.

"Mornin', yourself," she replied, mimicking his drawl. He stepped into her living room and immediately the room seemed smaller.

"You look great," Jarratt said as he surveyed her bare shoulders and legs in the yellow sundress. "I was beginning to think that you didn't have legs," Jarratt teased, referring to her uniform pants.

"Yes, I have legs, two of them," she replied lightly. Cassandra self-consciously gathered up her purse and sunglasses. "Would you like a cup of coffee before we go? I have some in the kitchen." Now that Jarratt was here, she was feeling a slight nervous twinge.

"No, thanks, room service treats me well," Jarratt said as he took her arm and they headed for the door. "I like your home," he added frankly as she locked her front door.

"Thank you, so do I," Cassandra replied as they walked toward the car and Jarratt opened the door for her.

"Where did you get that fabulous collection of furniture?" Jarratt asked.

"All over, but mostly in the East," Cassandra replied. "I love antiques."

"Some of those pieces would look fabulous in my house," Jarratt said as he started the engine. "The ranch house was built in 1890," he continued as he drove down her street and toward a main thoroughfare. "Subsequent generations didn't like the old furniture and got rid of most of it, but I love the old pieces and someday, when I have the time, I intend to redecorate the house in period furniture."

"Sounds lovely." Cassandra smiled as she pulled on her sunglasses. She tried to imagine how her antiques, most of them late Victorian, would look in a house of the era. She wished that she could see Jarratt's house and her furniture in it! She allowed herself a short daydream—his house, her furniture, their children . . .

"Where are we going today?" Cassandra asked brightly to banish the daydream that was becoming lovelier by the minute.

"I want to see Hoover Dam and take the guided tour," Jarratt said firmly, as though expecting her to argue.

"Sounds fine to me," Cassandra said mildly. And it did. The dam and power plant were well worth a trip to see.

"Oh," Jarratt replied. "I thought you might want to do something more glamorous."

"I do something glamorous every day of the week," Cassandra replied dryly. "Sometimes it's a relief to do something ordinary."

Jarratt looked at her in surprise. "I would have thought you loved the glamor and the sophistication. You made it your life's work, didn't you?"

Cassandra looked at him resentfully. "Just because I'm in a so-called glamorous profession, it doesn't mean that I can't enjoy simple things too."

"Sorry," Jarratt replied, aware that he had touched a nerve. "But you like it, don't you?" he asked again.

Cassandra bit her lip in indecision. Should she confide in Jarratt, tell him just how she felt about her job and her life? It would feel good to get it off her chest, but maybe Jarratt would find her as shallow as she found herself if she told him the truth. Or he might think that she was ungrateful for a well-paying job in these troubled economic times. And then, a man with so much purpose in his life probably wouldn't understand why she felt she had none. No, she would resist the temptation to cry on Jarratt's shoulder. "Sure, I like it," she said finally.

Jarratt took the highway that led out of the city, and they drove up the hills that would lead them to the dam. Las Vegas was located in a desert valley, and just to the southeast the Colorado River had carved a gorge between two mountains that was deep enough to build one of the foremost dams and hydroelectric plants in the country. Cassandra had toured the plant at least once a year with friends and relatives from Minnesota, and although she knew the tour almost by heart, she did not mind going. As they approached the dam, they could look down and see the churning waters of the Colorado River, leaping and foaming nearly 750 feet below them. Jarratt drove over the narrow highway that ran across the top of the dam, where Lake Mead lapped the wall on one side of the road and the huge dropoff could be seen over the other side, and parked in the visitor's lot by the lake. They walked to the entrance and he purchased tickets, and soon they were following the tour guide into an elevator that would carry them deep into the dam itself. Jarratt was amazed, as Cassandra had been the first time she had taken the tour, that the dam housed a number of underground offices and that they would be able to go down to the bottom.

As the tour guide took them deeper and deeper into the dam, Cassandra began to feel a little uneasy, especially as the vibration of the floors and walls due to the rushing water became more pronounced. Without meaning to, she slipped her hand into Jarratt's and was rewarded with a reassuring squeeze. Jarratt did not seem to share her discomfort, peering around the interior with curiosity and asking penetrating questions of the guide. Finally they reached the bottom of the dam and were taken into the viewing room where they could see the huge pipes that carried the water to the generators. As the tour guide explained, the water did not go through a hole in the dam or under it, but was actually channeled through huge conduits cut into the mountains on either side of the dam, that structure extending deep into the riverbed. As Cassandra pressed her nose up to the glass, she could both feel the rushing vibration of the water and hear its deafening roar. Jarratt peered out the window with her, his chin resting on top of her head in easy camaraderie.

The guide ushered the group out of the dam and into the generating plant itself. The huge turbine generators, as large as a house, gave no hint as to what was happening inside them, but Cassandra knew that whirling blades were creating electricity for much of Nevada and southern California. Jarratt pulled out a camera and posed her in front of a generator, explaining that a photograph would not have much impact unless there was someone standing by the generator to show how large it was. The tour guide herded the group toward the elevator and a quick ascent that left Cassandra's ears popping brought them back up to the top.

"How about some lunch?" Jarratt asked as he unlocked his car door.

"Sounds great, I'm starved," Cassandra admitted. It was nearly two and the coffee and toast she had eaten that morning had not lasted for very long. She turned to Jarratt expectantly. "Where do you want to go?" she asked, prepared to give him directions.

"Why don't I surprise you?" Jarratt asked lightly. Cassandra nodded. Instead of turning back toward the city, Jarratt consulted a map and headed up toward the main body of the lake. Cassandra assumed that he had selected one of the many lakeside restaurants to visit.

As they rounded the bend Cassandra could hear Jarratt gasp at the sheer size of Lake Mead. Down by the dam the vastness of the lake could not be seen or appreciated, but once they had gone around the blocking mountains, Mead could be seen in all her glory. Cassandra did not blame Jarratt for gasping. The sight was awesome. He drove for a few miles down the shore, then stopped at a particularly beautiful spot, with cool water lapping the shore in tranquil rhythm. "How's this for a picnic?" he asked.

"A picnic?" Cassandra squealed. "Where on earth did you come up with a picnic on the Strip?"

"I bribed the kitchen," Jarratt said dryly as he pulled out a large picnic hamper and a hotel blanket. Cassandra followed him to the little beach, and together they spread the blanket and sat down together. Jarratt placed the picnic basket between them, and Cassandra thrust her hand inside and brought up a plastic container of delicious fried chicken wings. Jarratt's hand followed hers, and withdrew a packet of thick roast beef sandwiches. "I think these are last night's hors d'oeuvres and prime roast," he said sardonically.

"Who cares?" Cassandra said breezily as she took one of the sandwiches from him and bit in. "This is delicious!" She handed him the chicken wings and he put a few on his plate, and together they made quick work of the hotel kitchen's early morning efforts. In addition to the sandwiches and chicken, the hotel had packed a rich pastry and an excellent bottle of white wine, which they desecrated by pouring into paper cups. As Jarratt gathered up the papers and packed the hotel's utensils, Cassandra poured them each another glass of wine and sat staring out at the water. She handed Jarratt his cup when he sat down beside her.

"What are you thinking?" he said in almost a whisper as she stared into the water.

"It's so peaceful," Cassandra breathed. "Sometimes I get hungry for some peace."

"I have that to spare back on the ranch," Jarratt admitted ruefully.

"Do you ever get tired of the ranch?" Cassandra asked, thinking of her own weariness with Las Vegas.

"Not at all," Jarratt reassured her firmly. "I like the bright lights for a few days, then I'm ready for the solitude." He laid back on the blanket and squinted into the sun. "How about you? Do you get tired of all the people? The noise?"

"I'm not sure," Cassandra admitted. She did not know for sure if it was the casino itself that was getting her down, or the other aspects of her life in Las Vegas. "I don't mind them," she added honestly. She turned her head and looked at Jarratt sprawled on the blanket, completely comfortable. His large body was warm and relaxed, and Cassandra resisted the temptation to run her hands down his sides and curl them around his waist. Jarratt's eyes were shut, so she could study him openly. His body was firm, hard, without an ounce of fat on it anywhere, and Cassandra knew from the intimate way that they had danced together that those muscles were strong and warm. A slight frown knit Cassandra's eyebrows. Last night Jarratt had not come in with her, even though she would have let him if he had wanted to. Now she was glad that he had not. But that was last night. Would tonight be different? Would he want to take her to his room tonight? Would she want him to, without being sorry in the morning? She did not treat making love lightly, but her feelings for Jarratt were different from those that she had felt for other men. Should she cast aside her restraint with Jarratt?

Jarratt swatted a fly and looked at his watch, jackknifing as he saw the time. "Good grief, it's after five!" he yelped. "The show is at eight!"

56

"Oops," Cassandra giggled as she jumped up. "I guess we better head back to town."

Quickly they folded the blanket and stuffed it and the basket back into the car. Jarratt drove back to the highway as quickly as he could on the narrow road, then stepped on the gas as they headed back into town.

"You better watch it," Cassandra cautioned Jarratt. "These state troopers around here will let you have it for that kind of speeding."

"But I have to drop you off, go get cleaned up, and pick you up again," Jarratt protested. "That's going to take some time."

"You don't have to do all that driving," Cassandra scoffed. "It will take me thirty minutes to get ready. You wait for me, and I'll pick up the tickets while you shower and change."

"Thirty minutes?" Jarratt asked doubtfully. "I never met a woman yet who could be ready in less than an hour!"

"Time me," Cassandra dared him, rising to the challenge. "I'll bet you the biggest desert on the menu."

"That's a bet," Jarratt said firmly as they entered the city.

He drove to her condominium, and Cassandra thrust open the door and raced toward the bathroom. She usually spent the hour that Jarratt estimated getting ready for an evening like tonight, but a bet was a bet, and Cassandra vowed that she would win.

She stripped off her sundress and panties and leaped into a lukewarm shower. She soaped herself quickly and squirted too much shampoo into her hair, making enough lather to wash Jarratt's hair too. She rinsed her hair under the spray, then grabbed a towel and dried herself as quickly as she could, wrapping her hair in another towel so she could deal with it later. She glanced at her alarm clock. Twelve minutes had passed. She had plenty of time.

Cassandra pulled on fresh panties and a pair of panty hose, almost snagging them in her haste. She reached into her closet and pulled out her most stunning cocktail dress —a red sheath with a plunging neckline and a slit halfway up her thigh. She pulled the dress over her head, grateful that she could not wear a bra with this dress and therefore did not have to take the time to put one on. She returned to the bathroom and pulled out her makeup drawer. Seventeen minutes. She still had time to do a complete makeup job. Feverishly she made up her eyes with shimmering gray shadow to match her irises, then applied a thin film of foundation and powder, finishing the look with a bright ruby lipstick and a bright blusher. She glanced at the clock. Three minutes. She grabbed a pair of shoes out of the closet, stuffed her wallet, keys, and lipstick into an evening bag, and grabbed a brush out of the bathroom. Whipping the towel off of her head, she slipped on a thick gold ring and her diamond pendant.

"I'm ready," she crowed, presenting herself to Jarratt in the living room. He had his feet propped up on the hassock and was reading a magazine.

"One minute to spare," he said as he turned around. "You're not ready after all!" he exclaimed triumphantly. "You can't leave now! Your hair's still wet!"

"That's quite all right," Cassandra said calmly. "It will dry in the car. I am ready to go."

"My God, I don't believe it," Jarratt breathed. "The bet's yours. Do you always get ready this quickly?"

Cassandra nodded and managed not to laugh out loud. As Jarratt walked her to the car, still shaking his head, she was grateful that she could put on a poker face when she had to.

* * *

Cassandra knocked gently on the door to Jarratt's suite. They had separated the minute they had reached the hotel, and Jarratt had gone up to change while Cassandra had stood in line and patiently waited for the tickets. She was pleased with Jarratt's choice. Wayne Newton always put on a good show, and she tried to catch him a couple of times a year if she could. Jarratt answered the door, bare to the waist and wearing a pair of dress pants, a damp towel slung around his neck and his raven hair still glistening from the shower. Wordlessly Cassandra stared in fascination at the broad chest covered with curly black hair that tapered to a V on his stomach, and the brawny shoulders that his shirts only hinted at. My God, what a magnificent man! Cassandra curled her fingers around the tickets in an effort to keep from throwing herself into Jarratt's arms. Instead, she wandered into the room as casually as she could and sat down in one of the plush chairs near the huge window. A round bed, covered in red velvet, dominated the room, and through the doorway to the bathroom Cassandra could see a small Jacuzzi. Although not as fancy as some of the hotel rooms in Las Vegas were reported to be, this one certainly was comfortable.

"Would you like a drink?" Jarratt asked.

"No, I don't think so," Cassandra said as she watched him pull a white shirt out of the closet. "We won't be here long enough to bother room service."

"Don't have to call them," Jarratt said as he pointed to a bar on the far side of the room. Cassandra wandered over and surveyed the bar, then laughed out loud. The bar had a series of buttons labeled with some of the more standard drinks. She reached out and pushed a couple of buttons, and in barely a moment a dumbwaiter opened to reveal a Scotch on the rocks and a glass of white wine.

"I thought I'd seen it all, but I think that takes the

cake," Cassandra admitted as she handed Jarratt his drink.

He swallowed a little, then set the glass down. "Can you help me with these damned cuffs?" he asked.

Cassandra bent to fasten the tiny studs. She was overpoweringly aware of the nearness of his strong, sensual body, and could smell his crisp aftershave and the elusive odor of his shampoo. As she fumbled with the second stud, Jarratt reached out and ran his hand lightly down her hair. "I couldn't believe the way you brushed your hair into those beautiful waves," he breathed as he stroked her shining locks. "I was sure that you had to spend hours on it."

Cassandra shook her head, her fingers laced together. Jarratt turned her into his arms and bent his lips to hers, crushing her to him and claiming her mouth violently. She met his passion with a rising sensuality of her own, moaning when his hand slid down her back and cupped her hip, pressing her into him so that she could feel the extent of his desire for her. She reached up on her tiptoes and locked her arms around his neck, gasping when Jarratt straightened and brought her up off the floor. He held her effortlessly so that she was in no danger of falling, and whirled her around slowly. She was not even aware that her shoes had slipped off, so caught up was she in the world of sensual pleasure they shared.

Jarratt released Cassandra gradually letting her slide slowly down his body and setting her down gently on the carpet. He looked at her with an unvoiced question in his eyes, a question that Cassandra understood but was not quite ready to answer. She smiled faintly and retrieved her shoes. "We better go on down to the show," she whispered.

Understanding that she was saying neither yes nor no, Jarratt nodded and pulled on his shoes, then slipped into his coat and found his key. Together they walked down to the lobby and took their place in line. As they waited for their table and all through dinner, Jarratt and Cassandra kept up a stream of bright small talk, evading the question that was in both of their minds. Jarratt cheerfully paid his bet with a huge dish of cherries jubilee that Cassandra ended up giving back to him anyway. As the curtain rose and the warm-up comic came out, Cassandra retreated into her thoughts, grateful for the respite.

With one part of her mind Cassandra enjoyed Wayne Newton thoroughly. He was a marvelous performer and tonight he was at his best. But another part of her mind was in turmoil. Should she go up to Jarratt's room with him? Should she let him make love to her? Cassandra started visibly as a new thought occurred to her. Was that what was eating her, the lack of male companionship in her life? Was the problem not Las Vegas after all, but just plain old loneliness?

Cassandra tumbled those thoughts around in her head for the entire length of the show. She was attracted to Jarratt and the feeling was clearly mutual. She wanted to go to bed with him, to feel his body unite with hers and to experience the ecstasy she knew they would share. He was a wonderful man, so different from most of the men she had known, and she knew that she could care for him, even if they had just two weeks to be together. *I need that,* Cassandra thought. *I need to be loved, to be cared for, even if it's just for a little while.*

Cassandra and Jarratt joined in the enthusiastic applause as Wayne Newton came out for several curtain calls. Jarratt took her arm as they walked out of the theater, smiling down with warm eyes that still had a question in them. Cassandra took a deep breath, smiled back at him, and nodded. Jarratt grinned openly and together they walked toward the elevator.

CHAPTER FOUR

Jarratt unlocked the door to his room and stood aside for Cassandra to enter. Stepping into the room, she felt a frisson of excitement in her stomach and she was suddenly ridiculously nervous. She wanted to go to bed with Jarratt and share with him the affection and warmth that she knew she would find with him. Yet, now that she had committed herself, she was a little unsure. Jarratt shut the door behind him and turned to Cassandra with a soft smile on his lips, touching her face gently with his fingers when he accurately read the nervous apprehension in her eyes. "This isn't your usual scene," he said softly, "is it?"

Cassandra shook her head. "No, it isn't," she replied simply.

"I'm glad," Jarratt replied as he took her hand.

"I'm going to get a drink. Want one?" he asked casually. Cassandra was surprised to note that his fingers were trembling. *Why, he's as nervous as I am!* she thought in amazement. For some reason that made him seem just that much more special.

"Sure," she replied softly. "A tequila sunrise if there's a button for one of those."

Jarratt released her hand and pushed the appropriate buttons on the dumbwaiter for their drinks. In a moment the marvelous contraption delivered Cassandra's drink and a Scotch for Jarratt. He handed her the tequila sunrise and sipped his Scotch slowly. "Would you like to relax in the Jacuzzi?" he asked.

"Sure," Cassandra replied as she sipped her drink.

Jarratt put his own drink on the end table and took Cassandra's from her, setting it beside his, then reached out and pulled her to him. He turned her around and slowly unzipped the slinky dress, then slid his fingers inside and gently eased it down her body, gliding his hands around and cupping her bare breasts in his curled palms for a moment. Cassandra gasped as his fingers found her button-hard nipples and feathered them lightly, making them tauten and tingle. Then his fingers returned to their task, pushing the dress down her body until she could step out of it. Quickly, deftly, he hooked his thumbs into her panty hose and slip, and in one smooth motion he peeled her slip, stockings, and panties from her body. Cassandra stared down in amazement at her suddenly naked form. "Where did you learn to do that?" she asked with genuine admiration.

"UT El Paso," Jarratt replied wickedly. "I belonged to the most interesting fraternity on campus." Still standing behind her, he bent his head and nuzzled her neck softly with his warm lips, sending quivers of delight down Cassandra's body. Suddenly she felt him tense and the tender sensations he had created inside her slowly ebb.

She turned in his arms and looked at him reassuringly. "It's okay. Everything is fine," she answered, reading accurately the question in his eyes. She was on the pill, even though there had been no need for her to be. But she had stayed on it, hoping that someday she would be able to share the intimacy she so desperately wanted with someone like Jarratt.

She undid his tie and threw it across the floor. Reaching up, she planted a kiss in the brown triangle of his throat that was exposed, then slowly moved down the front of his shirt, flicking open the buttons one by one, revealing inch after inch of his hard, brown chest.

When she reached the waistband of his trousers he reached out and stilled her hand. "You'll break your fingernails," he said softly, taking her hand to his mouth and kissing her well-manicured fingers softly. "Let me." He removed his own pants as quickly as he had her underwear and stood before her, then reached out and held her in front of him by the shoulders, drinking in the sight of her lush, curvaceous body. "Perfect, absolutely perfect," he breathed as he reached down and touched the tip of one of her breasts with his tongue.

"Likewise," Cassandra replied simply as she saw his naked body for the first time. Lean and hard, Jarratt did not have the kind of muscles that a man acquired by working out three times a week at the local spa. He had the tough, strong body of a workingman, with huge brawny muscles in his chest and arms and carved strength in his legs and thighs. Faint tan lines showed across his arms and around his neck, and his legs were a shade lighter than his arms and face, indicating that he spent most of his time in the sun actually working, but if anything the lines simply added to his appeal. Faint scars from injuries probably acquired on the ranch marked his arms and legs. Fascinated by him, Cassandra reached out and ran her hand down his chest and onto his stomach, finding the outline of his sinewy muscles under her fingers almost unbearably exciting.

"Come on, woman," Jarratt commanded as his stomach muscles tightened under her touch. "Let's go get wet." He took her by the hand and led her into the bathroom, where the Jacuzzi, just big enough for two, was bubbling merrily. Jarratt stepped into the swirling water, then turned and extended his hand to Cassandra. Slowly she climbed in, exclaiming in delight as the warm water caressed her naked body. They sank down in the water up to their necks, lying side by side in the frothing bubbles.

"This is wonderful," Cassandra cooed, her earlier nervousness forgotten. Relaxing with Jarratt in the warm water, she reached out and ran her toes down his leg.

"Watch it, Cassandra," Jarratt replied, his head against the side of the tub, his eyes closed. "That tickles."

"What tickles?" she asked, snaking her toe up just a little bit higher.

"Your toe," he replied laconically, not opening his eyes.

"What toe?" she asked impishly, running her toe up over his thigh.

"*This* toe!" Jarratt growled, grabbing her foot and tickling it as Cassandra laughed helplessly. He grasped her around the waist and pulled her on top of him in the water, holding her on his stomach, her face a mere inch from his. "I'm going to have to repay you for that," he said softly as he put his hand on the back of her head and pushed her mouth down on his.

They had kissed before, but never with this kind of freedom. Their mouths locked together; they savored each other's sweetness, each tasting the essence of the other. Their bodies were crushed together, and Cassandra could feel every inch of his hard, warm contours as the bubbles caressed them gently. Not letting go of her mouth, Jarratt's hands found their way down her body slowly, exciting her with their gentle touch. He explored her sensitive neck and her swelling breasts, causing them to come alive at the touch of his fingers. He fanned his hand across her stomach and found her soft hips, tickling them softly with a feather-light caress.

Cassandra pulled her head up and stared into Jarratt's face. This close, she could see the fine network of lines that framed his eyes, lines that he had earned from long hours of squinting into the sun. She looked into those dark eyes

65

and he gazed into hers wordlessly, then she bent her head and nibbled the brown skin of his strong neck, finding an earlobe and running her tongue around it. Her fingers tangled in the warm, wet hair on his chest, and she let her hands and eyes explore his body until it was as familiar to her as her own. With her own eyes she saw the evidence that Jarratt found her as exciting as she found him. But neither of them was in a hurry. It was as though they wanted to savor the moments before they were united for as long as they could, as though by prolonging their anticipation they could heighten their ecstasy.

Jarratt half-turned in the water and took one of Cassandra's breasts in his hand, lifting it so that he could reach it with his mouth. With gentle, sensitive lips he teased it, then found her other breast and caressed it, too, as she moaned with pleasure. Cassandra licked the perspiration off her upper lip as she drowned in the wild sensation he was arousing in her. No man had ever made her feel this way with just the touch of his fingers and lips.

Jarratt slid his arm under her and lifted her up from the foaming water. "We'll come back in a little while," he promised as he stood her on the furry bath rug and joined her there. Gently, tenderly, he rubbed her dry with a towel, then toweled his own body quickly. Tingling from head to toe, Cassandra watched him impatiently, desire darkening her gray eyes. "Come on," Jarratt said as he whisked her off her feet and carried her to the round bed. Without bothering to turn back the covers, he laid Cassandra down in the middle and joined her on the red fur bedspread.

Cassandra reached for Jarratt and touched him with loving hands. He took her in his arms and caressed her body gently, roughly, excitingly, as though he couldn't get enough of just touching her. *It's never been like this before,* Cassandra thought in wonder as Jarratt led her higher and

66

higher to a place somewhere beyond the sun. How much more of this exquisite pleasure could she take? Jarratt whispered, and she nodded, and when he made them one she thought she would cry out with delight. Maybe she did, she wasn't sure, so lost were they in the world of beauty that they were bringing to each other. Every inch of her body was singing, dancing, moving with the essence of his as they savored the joy of their union. They were rough, they were gentle, they were playful, they were intense; they explored all facets of each other's pleasure. When Cassandra reached the blinding moment of fulfillment, she arched her back and whimpered Jarratt's name in a hoarse whisper, shuddering in the throes of passion. Groaning, Jarratt joined her there, then they clung together as they slowly descended into reality.

"Cassandra?" Jarratt drawled quietly, sipping his watery drink, diluted by the melted ice cubes.

"Yes, Jarratt?" Cassandra replied, nestling her head on his shoulder and stretching her legs in the bubbling froth. They had lain, spent, on the bed for long moments as their pulses had slowed and their breathing returned to normal, then Jarratt had swept her up and carried her back to the Jacuzzi. He had retrieved their drinks from the end table and had joined Cassandra in the soothing water.

"What happened in there . . . well, is it always . . . was it—" Jarratt stammered.

"No, Jarratt, it isn't always like that for me," Cassandra replied steadily as she sat up and crossed her legs in front of her. Sipping her watered-down drink, she smiled at him shyly. "In fact, it's never been like that for me before," she admitted as a telltale blush crept up her face.

"Me either," Jarratt admitted as he splashed his legs in the water a little. He shook his head in wonder. "Never."

"I guess we had something special," Cassandra said softly, smiling a sad, mysterious smile.

"Had, woman? Did you say *had*?" Jarratt asked forcefully as he stood up and pulled her with him, holding her close and kissing her passionately. In spite of her extreme satisfaction of just moments before, Cassandra felt excitement begin to lick through her veins at the touch of Jarratt's warm, wet body on hers, and she ran her arms around his hard waist in delighted anticipation.

"Have, Jarratt. Have," Cassandra amended as he swept her off of her feet and carried her back to the bed.

What is wrong with me? Cassandra asked herself as she ran her agitated fingers through the tousled brown curls on her forehead and gulped a swallow of too-hot coffee. The burning liquid scalded the inside of her mouth, but she couldn't very well spit it out in the break room, so she swished it around a little and swallowed it the minute it was cool enough to go down. Blowing on the coffee in the foam cup, she gave it a moment to cool and sipped it cautiously, scowling at her image in the mirror on the wall. *I'm supposed to look all tired and satisfied,* she thought as she took in her tense face with the dark circles under her eyes. Well, she did look tired. As well she ought to. She and Jarratt had made love until dawn, then she had left him sleeping in the big round bed and called a cab from the lobby, riding home as the sun came up over the sandy desert city. She had fallen into an exhausted slumber, waking three hours later barely in time to dress and show up at the casino by noon.

But satisfied? She certainly didn't look that! *And I don't know why,* Cassandra thought as she looked again at her tense, strained face. Jarratt had satisfied her again and again, drawing a sensual response from her that she had never even dreamed she was capable of. As he lifted her to the heights time after time, she marveled at the chord they had struck in each other, for Cassandra knew that she had brought the same astounding satisfaction to him that he had given her. So what was the matter with her today?

Listlessly she threw the cup, coffee and all, into the trash can and trudged back out to her table. Automatically she shuffled the cards and began to deal. By the third hand she could tell that none of the people at her table were very good gamblers and she knew that she would not have to concentrate on winning against them, so she dealt automatically and studied the people around her, searching for any clue as to why she was so out of sorts. After a night like last night, she ought to be the most satisfied woman in Las Vegas!

Cassandra smiled and nodded as a new couple joined her table. Young, in love with each other, they stood side by side, the gleam of brand-new wedding bands on their fingers. They spoke with the soft accents of the Deep South, and from the way they kept looking at each other, they were obviously on their honeymoon. Cassandra had seen literally thousands of honeymooners over the years, and had always looked upon them with tolerant amusement, but today she stared at the couple and was amazed to feel jealousy for the young girl clawing at her insides. She had never felt that way before, but she was actually envious of the young bride. Why? Cassandra asked herself, baffled, as she automatically dealt the cards. The couple played a few rounds, then realizing that they were way out of their league, paid up cheerfully and wandered away, leaving Cassandra staring after them as they disappeared into the crowd.

She won't have to say good-bye to him in two weeks, Cassandra thought as a fresh wave of jealousy attacked her. *She has him for the rest of her life, and she knows it.* Suddenly the truth hit Cassandra with such force that she dropped the pack of cards that she was shuffling and had to start over. She actually wanted what that girl had! She wanted security, a home life, a permanent relationship. This can't be good old Cassandra, she marveled, one-day-at-a-time no-strings-attached Cassandra. But it was! She actually found herself longing for the security and the warmth of a permanent relationship with a man. Marriage? Did she want marriage? Cassandra mulled over that thought as she dealt for the last few minutes of her floor time, then she fled to the break room, her mind whirling. Spending the night with Jarratt, sharing warmth and affection as well as physical pleasure with him had released a whole Pandora's box of emotions and feelings that she had been trying for months to ignore. But she could ignore them no longer. She hated her life in Las Vegas. There! She had admitted it. She wanted something else, something secure, permanent, meaningful. She *had* to find something else before the restlessness and the dissatisfaction ate her alive.

Propping her feet up on the couch, she shut out the sounds of the other dealers laughing and talking and thought about her future. What options did she have? Could she get married? That was a life-style that Cassandra had never even considered for herself before, but it was possible, she guessed. But to whom? Jarratt's handsome face swam into Cassandra's mind and she thought about him. She wasn't in love with him, at least not yet, and he probably considered her no more than a vacation fling. Yet the passion that they had shared last night had been something that a person might find once in a lifetime, if he or she were lucky. But even if the impossible happened and Jarratt or someone like him did ask her to marry him, would she ever be able to fit into a life-style like his, or any life-style other than the one she led in Las Vegas? She just didn't know, and that worried her. Pushing thoughts of

70

marriage aside, she thought about trying to find another job. But what could she do except deal cards? If she wanted to do something else for a living that would pay anywhere near what dealing paid, she was going to have to get some training of some sort. But what on earth would she train for? Besides, no job could give her the love and security that she craved. *Oh, Cassandra, you picked a fine time to go and get unhappy with your life,* she chided herself. Annoyed, she ruffled the hair on her forehead and plopped her feet on the floor. She was going to have to make a change of some kind in her life, that was for sure. She couldn't go on like this for much longer. But what kind of change would make her happy?

Worried and frustrated, Cassandra returned to the pit for the final hour of her shift. Without looking at the people standing at her table, she shuffled the deck and dealt the cards, playing the hand automatically as she pictured herself in various different life-styles. Would she enjoy a service profession, such as nursing or teaching? As she collected chips from all but the player in second base, she imagined herself in a classroom full of wiggling kindergartners on a rainy day. *No, Cassandra,* she thought as she dealt another hand, *you don't want to do that!* Again collecting chips from everyone but the player in second base, she gave him the chips that he had won and dealt again. A nurse? Cassandra imagined herself in a white uniform standing in the operating room. Yes, she thought, that might be something to look into. She pictured herself standing beside the doctor, swathed in hospital garb, solemnly handing him the scalpel. The doctor, who was in love with her, of course, would reach out and make an incision . . .

No, Cassandra thought as she collected chips from all but the one player at her table. Not nursing. She hated the sight of blood! Sighing, she paid the player in second base

71

his winnings, a rather larger amount this time, and prepared to deal again. An airline hostess? Too old, you had to be in your twenties to attend the flight attendant training. She dealt the cards again, her mind about to go off on another tangent, when she noticed Joe, the pit boss, glower at the man in second base and then look at her strangely. What is the matter with Joe? she wondered as the people at her table played their hands. The man in second base asked for another card and she dealt it to him. He glanced at the card, raising his head a little, and the shock of recognition literally stunned Cassandra. The man was none other than Buddy Thomas, one of the best and most dreaded "players" in Vegas.

Buddy must know every system in the book, Cassandra thought bitterly as she paid him his winnings and dealt another round. He came to the casinos regularly, driving up in his white Bentley and leaving several hours later and several hundred thousand dollars richer. The dealers hated him, because he drove their PC's down, they lost money on their tips, and some of his victims had been given lower limit tables by frustrated pit bosses. As he asked for another card he smiled sheepishly at Cassandra, as though he knew what was going on in her mind, and she had to smile inwardly at the irony. Jarratt had the looks and the style to be a professional gambler, yet he didn't gamble. Buddy was maybe as tall as Cassandra, paunchy, and had freckles and a receding hairline, yet he was a menace at the blackjack table. Cassandra knew that if she intended to keep her PC up, she was going to have to concentrate on nothing else but beating Buddy for the next few minutes. Perspiration beaded her upper lip, and her mind, exhausted by the lack of sleep and the thoughts that had been whirling around in it all day, felt as though it had been wrapped in cotton.

Buddy won the next three games easily, betting and

winning larger amounts of money each time. Cassandra concentrated with all that she was worth and managed to beat him on the next two games, but he came back with four in a row and, with the amount of money that he was betting, her PC was falling drastically. *Damn, I wish I could count,* Cassandra thought angrily, *I'd show this cheating bastard.* Inwardly she cursed the pride and self-respect that had kept her honest. As usual for someone on a winning streak, Buddy had attracted a large crowd of lookers who were cheering for him, and although she could not see them, she knew that the "eye in the sky," pit security, was directly above them on the catwalk, binoculars in hand, watching every move that she and Buddy made. *Come on, Cassandra,* she thought, *you can do it.*

As she dealt another hand she glanced to her left to see if Joe was still watching the proceedings, and spotted Jarratt watching her silently from a few feet away, a look of tender concern on his face when he saw the angry desperation in hers. As her eyes widened he gave her a sudden thumbs-up sign, and her spirits buoyed considerably before she took another card from the deck. She had twenty, Buddy only nineteen. Dealer's hand!

At that point Cassandra's confidence, which had taken such a beating on the earlier games, returned in full force. She collected Buddy's chips, which amounted to a considerable amount of money, and dealt again. She pitted her instinct and her honest skill against Buddy's counting system, and although he had the theoretical edge, Cassandra begin to win more and more of the casino's money back from him. They played game after game, the other players at the table merely props for Buddy and Cassandra, who were deadlocked in a dead heat. Finally, as the pit security came around to unlock the drop box, Buddy shrugged and laid down his cards. Wordlessly he gathered up his pile of chips, considerably smaller than it had been at one point during the evening, and walked toward the cashier's cage. The crowd of lookers melted away and the eye in the sky left her table and resumed a normal patrol. Cassandra gratefully relinquished the table to her relief and walked, tired, out of the pit.

"That wasn't bad, Cassandra," Joe said as she passed by his table. "I'm glad you didn't dump that game."

"So am I," Cassandra said dryly, although she knew that Buddy had lowered her PC some. "You'd have put me on a nickel table for sure."

"Now, you know I wouldn't have put you on a five-dollar table," Joe said soothingly. "A ten, yes." He grinned and winked broadly, but Cassandra was not fooled. If she had not rallied, he would have busted her to a lower limit table, and they both knew it.

Jarratt was waiting for her at the door of the break room. "What was going on?" he asked as Cassandra smiled up at him wearily.

"It's a long story," she admitted. "How are you tonight?" she asked, feeling ridiculously shy as she remembered the intimacy and the passion they had shared.

"I'm wonderful," Jarratt said softly, a warm glow in his eyes. "But I woke up this morning and you weren't there."

"I went home and slept a little," Cassandra admitted, brushing a strand of hair from her eye.

"Go get your purse and I'll feed you dinner," Jarratt commanded softly.

Cassandra hurried into the break room and grabbed the dress she had brought with her out of her locker. Knowing that Jarratt would be back tonight, she had brought a nice dress with her, a knee-length peach with a daringly plunging neckline. She went into the restroom and changed quickly, freshening her makeup a little at the crowded mirror and putting on a pair of panty hose and shoes.

After she stuffed her uniform into her locker, she joined Jarratt and, hand in hand, they walked to his car. "I'd like to do something a little different," he said. "Have any ideas?"

"Would you like to see some snow?" Cassandra asked.

"We don't have time to fly to Tahoe tonight," Jarratt replied teasingly. "Somewhere closer."

"Ah, but there is snow closer," Cassandra replied. "About forty-five minutes away."

"Are you serious?" Jarratt asked.

"Sure am," Cassandra said as Jarratt opened the door to the car for her. "Take the highway north out of town."

She gave him detailed instructions and soon they were on the highway that led to Charleston Peak. Jarratt concentrated on his driving and Cassandra snuggled down into her seat, watching him as she relived those hours of delight that she had spent in his arms. In his presence the frustration and the discontent that she had felt all day miraculously faded away, to be replaced by a satisfied contentment, a feeling of belonging. Just being near Jarratt made everything seem all right.

"Good grief, it really is snow," Jarratt exclaimed as they drove high up the mountain peak. "When do the snowfalls start?"

"Mount Charleston has snow pretty much year round," Cassandra said as they pulled up in front of the quiet, rustic restaurant that nestled near the top of the mountain. "Pretty hard for a Texan to believe, isn't it?"

"Yes, it is," Jarratt admitted. "We do get snow sometimes in west Texas, but it isn't common." He killed the engine and got out of the car. "But the air's not that cold!" he exclaimed as he held the door for Cassandra.

"I know that," she replied. "I don't understand it either. A weatherman I'm not."

The young, smiling headwaiter escorted Jarratt and

Cassandra to their table and handed them menus. After they had both ordered a large steak, Jarratt leaned back and slowly and sensually stripped Cassandra with his eyes, remembering the way she had looked in his Jacuzzi last night, letting Cassandra know exactly what he was thinking without saying a word. She returned his smoldering gaze, recalling every inch of his hard, muscular body and the way it had felt crushed against her feminine softness. They would be together again tonight, that was sure. Her earlier tiredness and dissatisfaction forgotten, Cassandra's eyes sparkled and her cheeks grew warm with anticipation.

The arrival of the salads brought an end to Cassandra's reverie. Suddenly hungrier than she had realized earlier, she dug into the dressing-drenched greens and sipped the wine that Jarratt had ordered for them. "What was going on at your table when I walked in?" Jarratt asked in puzzlement.

"I had a professional player on my table," Cassandra said evenly, her earlier near-panic gone. "He's one of the best in Las Vegas. He's caused more dealers to dump games and get busted to lower tables than any other gambler on the strip. Most of us cringe when we see him coming."

"I thought you did pretty well," Jarratt commented as he downed a forkful of salad.

"I hadn't been until you came along," Cassandra replied honestly. "I was losing badly. My mind wasn't on the game."

"Where was your mind?" Jarratt asked wickedly. "Happy memories?"

"Yes, damn you, that was part of it," Cassandra replied dryly. Her face clouded a little. "But not all of it," she added almost to herself.

"Not all of it?" Jarratt asked in mock indignation. His face softened. "Is there anything else bothering you?"

Isn't there, though, Cassandra thought to herself as the waiter placed their juicy steaks in front of them. Jarratt immediately tackled the huge steak, and Cassandra was grateful for the interruption that gave her time to think. Should she tell Jarratt about her discontent with her lifestyle? She had thought about telling him once but had decided against it. Should she say something now? Cassandra bit into her juicy steak and studied Jarratt as he ate. Although in some ways they were as close as two people could be, in other ways they were still very much strangers. Besides, Jarratt might not want to spend his evening hearing all about her problems. He was on vacation, they were having a romance, and she certainly didn't want to spoil that for him. He might think that she was hinting around for something if she told him how deeply she longed for a home and security. No, she wouldn't say anything to Jarratt. She would make his holiday romance something to remember, then after he left she would try to deal with what was happening in her life.

Thankfully Jarratt forgot about his question by the time he had finished his steak. They talked about all kinds of things, they laughed together, and as the evening wore on so did the sense of anticipation. A fine thread of tension wound itself tighter and tighter around the two of them, binding them together although physically they were separated by the dining table. Finally Jarratt picked up the check and helped Cassandra from her chair, then he paid the bill and they left the restaurant. The temperature had fallen, and Cassandra shivered beneath the lightweight coat that she wore. Jarratt reached out and pulled her to his side, holding her close and rubbing her arm with his to lend it some warmth. Together they stared up at the sky, marveling in soft whispers at the brightness of the twinkling stars.

"I never see stars like this unless I come up here," Cassandra said wistfully. "The lights in Las Vegas pretty well overpower them."

"You can still see them from my front porch," Jarratt said softly as he kissed Cassandra's temple gently.

"I guess you can, can't you?" Cassandra said quietly. "Do you ever have time to look at them?"

"Of course," Jarratt replied as he rubbed Cassandra's arm absently. "I make it a point to go out for a few minutes every night and just look at the sky. It restores me."

"Lucky man," Cassandra murmured as a sweet longing pierced through her being. Oh, how she wished that she could stand with Jarratt on his front porch and stare at the stars in the sky! Cassandra felt an emotion almost akin to homesickness as she gazed upward, even though she had never ever been to Texas, much less to Jarratt's ranch. *Maybe it's Jarratt,* she thought. *Maybe it's because I want to be with him. Yes, that's it,* she realized suddenly. It was a longing for the man, not the place, that had her in its grip.

Jarratt turned Cassandra in his arms so that she was facing him. Her breath made a small white cloud as she pursed her lips and breathed out his name softly. Swaying toward her, he reached out and captured her willing lips with his own, his lips cool and tasting of white wine. Cassandra looped her arms around his neck and melted into him, the pressure of her mouth against his warming him and sending chills down to the tips of her toes. Remembering the ecstasy of last night, her body screamed for Jarratt's to possess her again, and she strained impatiently against the clothing that they both wore. Reluctantly Jarratt broke the kiss, looking at her with

78

smoldering passion in his dark eyes. "You will stay with me again tonight," he said. It was a statement, not a question.

"Yes, of course," Cassandra replied. "Or better yet," she said simply. "You stay with me. I make a mean pot of coffee in the morning."

Jarratt reached down and kissed her once, hard, on the lips. "Your place it is, then," he said softly. "It's going to be a wonderful two weeks, Cassandra," he added as he took her hand and ran with her to the car.

CHAPTER FIVE

Cassandra sighed and poured herself another cup of coffee. Life was so wonderful! She was in love for the first time in her life, and her future stretched out before her like a bright red ribbon. *Oh, Jarratt, I love you,* she thought as she drank her coffee and put her dishes into the sink. *And I know that you love me, too.* Almost running, she hurried to her bedroom and packed a swimsuit and a towel in a tote bag. Jarratt had gone to check out of his hotel, but they had the entire day together before he had to fly back to El Paso. Cassandra laughed as she took in the rumpled sheets on the fourposter. Jarratt's hotel room certainly had not gotten much use this trip!

Jarratt and Cassandra had been inseparable for the last two weeks. Jarratt had wandered around the casinos while she was working, but they had spent every other minute together, and had shared the same bed every night, making love passionately until the wee hours of the morning, then clinging to each other as they slept contentedly in each other's arms. Cassandra had fallen deeply, irrevocably in love with Jarratt, and although he had not come out and said so yet, he gave his love away in a thousand little ways, from the way he touched her with such tender passion to the way he talked to her for hours on end, exploring every facet of her personality. He in turn had opened up with her, sharing himself in a way that Cassandra suspected he had never done with any other woman. *We have a once-in-a-lifetime love,* Cassandra thought contentedly. *And today he's going to propose. We will be married very soon, and we'll spend the rest of our lives together on his ranch.* Cassandra hugged herself tightly and grinned a silly grin. *And my life will be so full,* she promised herself, *loving Jarratt and taking care of his home and having his children.* Suddenly her life had become meaningful, and would be as fulfilling as she could ever wish. Glancing at the clock, Cassandra gasped and grabbed her jeans and shirt and threw them on. Jarratt had chartered a boat on Lake Mead and had promised her a special surprise. *Some surprise!* Cassandra thought. *He's going to propose, and he thinks I don't know it!*

Jarratt rang the bell as Cassandra pulled on a sneaker. Hopping to the door, Cassandra managed to open it and pull on the shoe at the same time, bringing a wide smile to Jarratt's face that grew into a laugh. He reached out and drew Cassandra to him, covering her mouth with his and kissing her in that tender, exciting way that she had so come to love. "Hello, woman," he whispered.

"Hello, yourself," Cassandra replied, kissing him again although they had been apart for only forty-five minutes. She grabbed her tote and together they locked the front door and climbed into Jarratt's rented car. The sun was warm, and they would be able to swim in the lake if they didn't stay in the water for too long. Laughing and chatting with him all the way to the lake, Cassandra said nothing about Jarratt's "surprise" and hoped she could pretend amazement when he popped the question.

The manager of the boat dock took them to the boat that Jarratt had chartered and showed them around. It was a small inboard with a tiny galley and an even smaller cabin with two twin-sized bunks on either side of a narrow passageway. The deck was large, though, and Cassandra

81

suspected that the boat was chartered for a lot of daytime outings. Jarratt paid the manager and stowed the picnic basket that he had brought from the hotel in the galley, then together they cast off the ropes and puttered out of the dock. Jarratt maintained a discreet speed until they were on the main body of the lake, then he opened the throttle and motored up the lake. The cool wind whipped Cassandra's hair into a taffy-colored cloud around her head and plastered her clothes to her body. The roar of the engine prevented conversation, but she and Jarratt shared a series of sweet, sensual smiles that said all that needed to be said. The lake water was almost a cobalt blue and the houses on the shore looked like a model village. They sped up the lake and Cassandra wondered where Jarratt had learned to handle a boat so skillfully.

They traveled up most of the main body of the lake until Jarratt spotted a fairly secluded but sunlit cove. He headed into it and killed the engine, dropping anchor in the middle of the cove. "We don't want to drift ashore while we're doing other things, now do we?" he asked wickedly as he threw the anchor over the side of the boat.

"Couldn't have that," Cassandra agreed. She stared up at the sky. "Did you ever see such a beautiful day?" she asked.

"No," Jarratt said softly, looking at her. "No, not ever." Cassandra was looking at the sky and missed the look of intense pain that fleetingly crossed his face.

"What do you want to do first?" Cassandra asked wickedly as she stood up and began to unbutton her blouse slowly.

Jarratt sat down and started to remove his sneakers. "What do you think?" he asked provocatively as he let his shoes drop, one at a time, on the wooden deck.

Although it had been only hours since they had made love, Cassandra could feel the excitement beginning to build in her again, and she stripped off her shirt slowly and deliberately, then unhooked her bra and let it fall to the deck. She kicked off her shoes as Jarratt stripped off his shirt and peeled off his pants and briefs. As Cassandra stepped out of the rest of her clothes, Jarratt reached out and she melted into his arms, swaying to claim his warm lips with hers. He reached out and placed his hands on her warm waist, then with startling speed he gripped her around the waist and picked her up, dropping her neatly over the side of the boat into the icy water. "I want to swim!" he shouted, jumping into the water right behind her.

Cassandra hit the water with a splat, gasping as the cold fluid surrounded her body, icy needles caressing every inch of her naked skin. "Damn you, Jarratt Vandenburg!" she sputtered as she broke the surface and gasped for breath. "This water's cold!"

"Naw, it ain't," Jarratt drawled teasingly. "Just a little cool, that's all." He laughed out loud as Cassandra sputtered indignantly. "Well, you did ask what I wanted to do," he reminded her innocently.

Cassandra replied by shoving a palmful of water into Jarratt's face. Momentarily stunned, he grinned wickedly and reached out and pushed Cassandra's head under the surface. She retaliated by reaching out and pulling the hair on his chest, refusing to let go even when he gave in and let her surface.

"Let go, woman," Jarratt growled as he tried to pry open her fingers. "Damn it, that hurts!"

"What, this?" Cassandra asked as she reached out and gave the hair another tug.

Jarratt reached out and pulled Cassandra to him, trapping her offending hand between their bodies and crushing it between them. He reached down and with cool, wet lips captured her mouth with his, drawing the sweetness from

83

hers. She gradually let go of the fistful of hair, curling her fingers into the tough muscles of Jarratt's chest. Together they clung, unmindful of the cold water, holding each other as only two lovers could. They sank slowly into the water, not breaking their embrace as the water enveloped them in its cold cocoon. Finally, light-headed, Jarratt broke the embrace and they kicked their way to the surface. They gasped for air until their lungs were full, then Cassandra broke away from him and swam briskly in circles around the boat.

They swam in the lake for the better part of an hour, stopping to kiss and caress each other often. Cassandra protested when Jarratt finally called a halt, but he pointed out that she was turning blue and that he preferred her in her usual pink state. As she climbed out of the water the breeze hit her bare skin and she shivered convulsively. Two strong arms lifted her from behind onto the deck, then Jarratt wrapped her in a thick towel that he found in the cabin. He dried her briskly and used a second towel on her hair, then pushed her toward the cabin. "Go get under the covers," he ordered her. "I'll join you as soon as I'm dry."

Shivering hard, Cassandra was only too glad to obey. She pulled back the cover and unwound the damp towel from her body. The sheets were unexpectedly rough to her skin, but the bunk was warm and she burrowed all the way under the covers, only her eyes and nose exposed to Jarratt when he joined her in the cabin.

"Shall I make love to you or tell you a fairy tale?" he teased as he unwrapped his towel. His body gleamed in the sunlight that streamed through the portholes, and his goose-pimpled skin was tan and vital.

"I don't care, just warm me up some," Cassandra said as she threw back the covers for Jarratt to join her. He climbed in, and for a moment she was disappointed. His skin was just as cold as hers was! Jarratt reached for her and held her close to his cool body, and gradually as they lay close and talked in loving whispers, their bodies warmed and they snuggled together comfortably. Cassandra lay her head on Jarratt's chest right above his heart and listened to the vaguely comforting sound of the strong beat under her ear. He rubbed the small of her back with his palm, soothing her and yet exciting her almost unbearably with his gentle touch. The boat rocked with the motion of the lake water, lulling Cassandra into a state that was not sleep, but a serene relaxation in which her mind was free to float, thinking about all things, yet nothing.

Just exactly when she and Jarratt crossed the line between relaxation and passion would have been hard to tell. At first they touched lightly, warmly, affectionately, seeking no response other than the contented sigh of affection. But gradually their caresses grew firmer, warmer, more passionate. Cassandra raised her head and sought Jarratt's lips with her own, covering his mouth with a series of short, light, feathering kisses that teased him. Jarratt's hand gradually slid lower and lower, finding her soft hip and caressing it gently as shooting sparks of pleasure shot through Cassandra's limbs, turning them to water. *He knows exactly where to touch me,* Cassandra thought as Jarratt continued his tender assault. Her fingers found the soft tuft of hair under Jarratt's arm and teased it lightly, then as he moaned softly she kissed his chest and neck as she had his mouth. She too knew where to touch Jarratt to draw forth his abandoned response.

Jarratt rolled her over and lay beside her so as to expose every inch of her body to his hungry hands and eyes. "Let me touch you," he murmured. "Let me see and caress every inch of your delicious body." He dipped his head and found her generous breast, tickling her nipple with his tongue in the way that he knew that she loved, watching

85

with tender love in his eyes as she wiggled in pleasure. His mouth moved to her sloping stomach and his tongue circled her navel in slow, tantalizing rhythm. His eyes and his hands feasted on her greedily, desperately, as though he could not get enough of her, and, driven by his desperation, Cassandra reached out and held him to her, tormenting his body as her hands found his firm hips and moved to stroke him lovingly, gently, and her lips caressed his neck. They gave of themselves eagerly, willingly, wantonly, each trying to give to the other the ultimate pleasure. *Oh, this is what it's going to be like for the rest of our lives,* Cassandra thought exultantly.

When Jarratt sensed that Cassandra was almost delirious with pleasure, he moved over her and made them one, claiming her sweetness with a firm possession that at the same time was incredibly loving and tender. Cassandra opened herself completely to him, giving passionately of herself yet greedily claiming Jarratt as her own. They moved together in complete harmony, instinctively yet with the grace and familiarity that had come from much loving. Knowing that Cassandra was about to reach the ultimate, Jarratt gathered her close as he moved with her, and, clinging together, they plunged over the edge of the precipice and sailed together on a free fall through space.

Thoroughly spent, they lay together wordlessly. *I wonder when he's going to ask me to marry him,* Cassandra mused as she lay on her back and stared at the ceiling. *Not that he's had a chance to! Oh, I can hardly wait.* Smiling, she promised herself that she would try to act surprised. Looking over at Jarratt, she was faintly disturbed to see a look of wistful longing rather than the sensual satisfaction that she had expected to see on his face. He was lying on his back and he had thrown his arm over his eyes in an almost protective gesture. "Jarratt?" she asked, worried.

Immediately the wistful look was replaced by a wicked grin. "You want more?" he asked.

"I don't see how," Cassandra replied wryly.

"Unfortunately you're right," Jarratt replied as he planted a hard kiss on her lips. "Even I am not without my limits." He swung his long legs out of the bunk and reached for the towel he had dropped on the floor. "I'll bring you your clothes," he volunteered as he climbed up the ladder. A moment later Jarratt, fully clothed, tossed Cassandra's clothes to her as he passed through the cabin to the galley. "Hungry?" he asked.

"Yes," Cassandra admitted as her stomach growled in agreement. Although she had eaten breakfast, the swim and the lovemaking had left her starved.

Jarratt was unpacking a veritable feast in the galley. He must have bribed the hotel kitchen well, for in addition to thick roast beef sandwiches, they had packed tubs of potato salad and an entire pound cake that Cassandra was certain had been baked fresh this morning. She unwrapped the food with trembling fingers, the anticipation almost unbearable. *I hope he proposes soon,* she thought. *The waiting is killing me!*

Jarratt, however, talked of everything else but marriage as they ate their portable feast. Not knowing what to think, Cassandra made the appropriate replies and tried to fight a feeling of dismay. Surely Jarratt was going to propose to her! He had to! They loved each other, and she was going to marry him and live with him on his ranch in Texas. She was going to have his love and live the fulfilling life with him that she wanted so much.

Cassandra dragged the meal out as much as she could, even eating a second piece of cake that she didn't really want, but Jarratt didn't say a word that vaguely resembled a proposal. Finally she began packing the picnic basket and putting the leftovers into a paper bag. What was wrong? Was Jarratt scared? Was he nervous? She washed up the utensils in the tiny sink while Jarratt wiped the table, then as she unplugged the sink Jarratt came up from behind her and slid his arms around her waist. "I have something for you," he whispered as he held a small jewelry box in front of her. "Your special surprise."

So this was it! Her engagement ring! And she was beginning to get worried! *Cassandra, how stupid can you be?* she asked herself. Slowly she reached out and took the little box and snapped open the lid. Inside, a small diamond heart on a chain winked brightly at her. "It's a parting gift," Jarratt said softly.

Cassandra turned to Jarratt with bewilderment and dismay on her face. Jarratt stared back at her with tears in his eyes. "This has been the best two weeks of my life," he told her with a thick voice. "I'll always remember you, Cassandra, and I want you to have something to remember me by." Before the stunned Cassandra could stop him, he had reached out and taken the necklace from the box and hooked it around her neck.

"But Jarratt, I don't understand," Cassandra whispered. "I love you."

"I love you too," Jarratt replied, holding her close. "I wanted you to have something really nice so that you won't forget me."

"But, Jarratt, this is all wrong," Cassandra said as she reached up to take off the necklace.

"No, leave it there," Jarratt commanded, stopping her hands with his. "I know you don't collect trinkets from men, but this one was given in love. I really want you to take it."

"It's not that," Cassandra replied, shaking her head. "Jarratt, this is all wrong! We love each other."

"Why is it wrong then?" Jarratt asked, backing away from her. "My giving you a necklace."

"It's not the necklace, it's the reason you're giving it," Cassandra replied through stiff lips. "You're saying good-bye."

Jarratt looked puzzled for a moment. "Of course I'm saying good-bye," he replied. "My plane leaves at six. I have to leave then." His face softened as he saw the distress in hers. "I can't stay forever, you know," he added quietly.

"I know that," Cassandra replied impatiently, pulling out a chair and straddling it. "You have to get back to your ranch."

"And you have to get back to your life in Las Vegas," Jarratt replied gently, touching her face tenderly with his fingers. "I've monopolized it terribly lately, I know."

"Oh, Jarratt, I didn't mind," Cassandra reassured him quickly. So that was it! He thought she would want to stay in Las Vegas rather than go with him. She looked up at him, her eyes full of love. "Look, that life in Vegas means nothing to me." She stopped and took a deep breath. "Did you think I wouldn't come to Texas with you?"

Jarratt looked confused. "Who said anything about you going to Texas?" he asked gruffly.

"Oh, Jarratt, it's all right!" Cassandra cried, jumping up from the chair. "You were afraid I wouldn't want to go to Texas with you, weren't you? That's the reason you didn't ask me to marry you. Oh, Jarratt, I would go anywhere on this earth to be with you. I thought you knew that." She wrapped her arms around his waist and held him close.

"Just a minute," Jarratt said firmly, removing her hands from his waist and sitting her down. "Are you seriously suggesting that you want to leave Las Vegas and come with me to Pecos? You have to be kidding!" he said firmly.

"And why do I have to be kidding?" Cassandra asked

89

impatiently. "You know I love you. And you love me; you said you did. So why can't we take it from there?"

"Because of you, and me, and Pecos, Texas, that's why!" Jarratt replied impatiently. He sat down on another chair and faced Cassandra. "Look, Cassandra, you've lived in the fun capital of the world for the last ten years. Instant entertainment. Instant parties. Instant fun. You name it, you could do it. Where I live it's a thirty-five-mile drive to Pecos, where you have the big choice of one café and a bar. The movie theater closed down a few years back. To see a movie you have to drive over a hundred miles. For entertainment we have a tall TV antenna, a few books, and a deck of cards. Besides, you have a fascinating job that you would miss."

"No, I wouldn't," Cassandra replied with spirit. "I'm sick of Las Vegas, Jarratt. I'd love to live on your ranch with you, honestly."

"You might last two days on the ranch," Jarratt replied flatly. "Then you'd be bored out of your gourd and begging me to take you somewhere, anywhere, to get away and have something to do. Look, I watched Mamacita and Dad go through years of it before Mamacita finally got fed up and left Dad and me for El Paso. And I didn't even blame her when she went. She was bored stiff. And if she was, I know you'd be."

"But, Jarratt, we can't just throw what's between us away!" Cassandra cried desperately. "My God, I've waited thirty-three years to find what we have together, and you're going to just give it all up because your parents didn't get along."

"My parents would have gotten along just fine if it hadn't been for the ranch," Jarratt replied angrily. "Dad couldn't change his life there and neither can I."

"Who's asking you to?" Cassandra replied impatiently.

"I told you, I don't care if I never deal another card in my life."

"That sure isn't the tune you've been singing for the last two weeks," Jarratt shot back. "Now all of a sudden you hate Las Vegas. If you're so sick of Vegas, why is this the first I've heard about it?"

"What was I supposed to do, ruin your vacation by griping about it? And then, when we fell in love, I thought that you would ask me to marry you and that I would be going to Texas with you. Oh, Jarratt, don't you love me at all?" Cassandra pleaded.

"Of course I love you," he replied with anguish in his voice, leaving his chair and pacing the room. "Why do you think I'm refusing to screw up our lives like you want to?"

"And why would we be screwing up our lives by getting married?" Cassandra demanded, facing him squarely in the middle of the galley.

"You know damn well what kind of chance we'd have," Jarratt snapped.

"Every couple takes a chance," Cassandra replied softly. "We wouldn't be taking any bigger chance than anybody else."

"Oh, Cassandra, come on," Jarratt replied with exasperation. "You know damn well what kind of a chance we'd be taking! Hayseed and the hothouse flower! That's just too big a gamble."

"And you're the one who won't gamble," Cassandra reminded herself slowly, turning away from Jarratt and staring out of a porthole. "You mean you're not even willing to gamble on something that's as important as our future together?"

"If I won't gamble my money, then I sure as hell won't gamble something as important as our futures," Jarratt said angrily.

"So you're willing to throw it all away instead," Cassandra said in wonder, turning back to face him. "Jarratt, no! We just can't do that! Why can't you take a chance on us?"

"Because every time I've ever gambled I've lost," Jarratt replied heavily. "This wouldn't be any different. Look, Cassandra, it's tearing my insides out to fly out of Las Vegas and leave you behind. But damn it, woman, it would hurt us both a lot worse to have to part after three months, or six months, or a year. I'm just trying to be reasonable."

"Reasonable, my foot," Cassandra snapped, throwing her head back and staring at him with glittering eyes. "You're just a coward." Jarratt's head flew up and he looked at her with a mixture of disbelief and anger. "Yes, you heard me. A coward. You're willing to throw it all away, not even give us a chance because we might not make it."

"And you just want a free ride out of Vegas because you're a little tired of it right now," Jarratt jeered. "Believe me, you'd be hightailing it back here soon enough."

The sound of Cassandra's hand connecting stingingly with the flesh on Jarratt's face startled them both. "That's a foul thing to say, and we both know it isn't true," she said through clenched teeth as Jarratt nursed his stinging jaw with his palm. "I can find my own way out." She looked at the clock on the wall and her eyes narrowed. "Look, I hate to break up this lovely argument, but your flight is for six and I'm sure you don't want to get your tailfeathers stuck in the cabin door, now do you?" she asked sweetly as she forced back tears.

Jarratt reached out and ran his hand down Cassandra's arm. She flinched away and turned on him angrily, tears pouring out of her eyes. "Don't you touch me, you bastard," she sobbed.

He sighed and looked at her sadly. "I'd marry you in

92

a minute if I thought there was any way I could," he said flatly. "I'm sorry, hon."

Jarratt had lifted anchor and they had motored back to the dock in silence, Cassandra sitting in the cabin and staring into space. In the car he had tried to speak to her, but she had cut him off and had turned her face to the window, refusing to give him another chance to further justify his actions. Determined not to cry in front of him again, she told him good-bye coolly at her curb, refusing to acknowledge the pain in his eyes or the catch in his voice when he bade her farewell. With a lump in her throat Cassandra had nodded briskly and slammed the car door shut behind her.

Cassandra let herself into the condominium and closed the door behind her, then collapsed on the couch and let the tears that she had been damming up inside her all afternoon flow. Choking on sobs, she cursed out loud, using every foul term that she had ever heard. Oh, why had Jarratt Vandenburg ever wandered into the Tropical Paradise? Why did she have to go and fall in love with him? *How could he just tell me good-bye like that?* Cassandra wondered as a fresh wave of tears flowed from her eyes and wet her elegant sofa. *I know he loves me just as much as I love him. Oh, Jarratt, I wish you had been willing to take a chance on me. We could have made it, damn you.*

Cassandra cried until her tears were spent, then listlessly she dragged herself to the bathroom, glancing at her tear-stained face in the mirror as she pulled the sticky clothes from her body and stepped under the cool spray. She let the water run over her body for long moments, trying to wash the feel and the scent of Jarratt from her, although she knew that she would never wash away the love that they had shared. Absently she reached up and fingered the diamond heart that circled her throat. It was beautiful, but she despised it nevertheless, because it had been Jarratt's way of saying good-bye to her.

As Cassandra stepped out of the shower she heard the telephone ringing. It was Jarratt! He had changed his mind and wanted her to come with him! Stumbling over her pile of clothes, she reached the telephone and picked up the receiver, only to hear a disconnect and the dial tone start. *Damn,* she thought. *I missed him. But he'll call back,* she promised herself. And as though to make her promise come true, the telephone immediately began ringing again.

"Jarratt?" Cassandra answered eagerly.

"Miss Howard, you don't know me, but I'm a friend of Sharon Burns. Your number is posted here by her telephone and I didn't know who else to call."

"What's wrong?" Cassandra asked anxiously, her own problems forgotten.

"Sharon's sick, real sick. Can you come over here?"

"Right away," Cassandra replied, slamming down the telephone and racing into a pair of jeans and a pullover top. Not bothering with her hair or makeup, she slid her feet into a pair of loafers and literally ran the block to Sharon's condominium.

Not bothering to knock, Cassandra threw open the door and immediately spotted Sharon lying on the couch moaning softly, and a paunchy middle-aged man leaning over her slapping her face lightly. "Wake up, honey, your friend's here."

"Don't want her," Sharon mumbled. "Just want to sleep." Her hair fanned out on the pillow and her face was a pasty white.

Cassandra elbowed the man out of the way and leaned over Sharon. "It's Cassandra," she called as she shook Sharon's arm gently. "Wake up, Sharon."

Sharon opened her eyes and looked at Cassandra blank-

94

ly. "Go away," she muttered. "I want to be left alone." She stared at Cassandra dully for a few seconds, then shut her eyes again, lapsing into unconsciousness.

"Call an ambulance," Cassandra told the middle-aged man. He stood there a moment dumbly, then turned and headed for the door.

"You call the ambulance," he said as he hurried out the door. "I don't want to be involved in this."

"Damn you to hell, then," Cassandra said out loud as she ran for the kitchen. She called for an ambulance, stressing the emergency nature of the situation, then looked around the kitchen and living room for some sign of what Sharon had taken, hoping that she could find some clue so that the doctors would know how to treat the sick woman.

The living room and the kitchen yielded nothing, but in the bathroom Cassandra hit the jackpot. On the counter sat two empty barbituate bottles and an empty fifth of Scotch. The sickening truth hit Cassandra with nauseating force. Sharon had tried to kill herself. And if that bastard who had found her had not happened along, she most likely would have succeeded. Cassandra returned to the living room and took Sharon's cold hand in hers and prayed for the ambulance to hurry.

The next few hours were a nightmare. Cassandra wrote down Sharon's parents' telephone number and followed the ambulance to the hospital in the Firebird. She answered the doctor's questions as best she could, then found a pay phone and placed a call to Sharon's parents in Missouri, telling them as gently as she could what apparently had happened and asking them to please come right away. Mrs. Burns, a sweet-sounding woman, broke down in tears over the phone, and Mr. Burns assured Cassandra that they would be there by morning. Then Cassandra found a coffee machine and sat in the waiting

95

room. She was bone-tired, but she couldn't very well leave until she knew that Sharon was going to be all right. All right physically, she amended to herself. Sharon hopefully would survive this attempt, but Cassandra wondered if the young woman would ever get over the effects of her slide into the fast lane. Damn Las Vegas anyway! This would never have happened if Sharon had stayed in Missouri.

About dawn a kindly nurse tapped on the shoulder of a dozing Cassandra. "Your friend is conscious and is asking for you," she said.

Cassandra sat bolt upright. "How is Sharon?" she demanded.

"We pumped her stomach and gave her some medication to neutralize the effects of the drugs that were already in her bloodstream, so she's going to be all right," the nurse assured Cassandra. She nodded gratefully as she followed the nurse to the intensive care unit. Sharon was hooked up to a myriad of machines and was still sickly pale, but her eyes were open and she recognized Cassandra.

"I'm sorry, Cass," Sharon whispered as her eyes filled with tears. "I just couldn't stand it anymore."

"Oh, Sharon, you don't have to apologize to me or anyone else," Cassandra replied heartbrokenly.

Sharon didn't appear to hear Cassandra's reassurances. "I just couldn't stand it anymore," she repeated almost to herself. Cassandra winced. "I got so tired. I just couldn't go on." Tears snaked down Sharon's face and dripped onto the cover.

"Sharon, I called your parents," Cassandra said quietly. "They'll be here soon."

"Oh, no!" Sharon cried. "Cassandra, how could you? How can I face my mother after what I've become?" The nurse looked at Cassandra warningly.

"Sharon, don't you ever say that about yourself," Cassandra replied forcefully. "Look, you made a mistake. Lots of young women do. But you can go back to Missouri and make a good life for yourself. Your mother loves you, and she would be the last person to hold a mistake against you."

"Do you really think so?" Sharon asked in a wobbling voice.

"I know so," Cassandra reassured her. She kissed Sharon on the cheek and left her to rest.

Of course, it wouldn't be that easy, Cassandra thought as she drove home in the early light of dawn. Sharon probably needed some professional help, and she might never completely forget the horror of the last few months in Las Vegas. "Damn it anyway!" Cassandra said out loud as she hit the steering wheel with her fist. "If she'd never come here, it never would have happened."

Once home, Cassandra pulled off her clothes and lay on the fourposter. Although it had been twenty-four hours since she had slept, her mind was whirling and sleep was the furthest thing from her mind. *I've had it with Las Vegas,* she thought, *and the kind of garbage that this place does to people. Damn it, I want to leave! I want to be with Jarratt!* She turned over and cradled the pillow in her arms, reeling with sensual longing when she caught a tantalizing whiff of Jarratt's aftershave on the pillowcase. *Oh, Jarratt, I want to be with you.*

So what was stopping her? Cassandra sat bolt upright in the bed. So Jarratt didn't think she would make it on his ranch! Well, she would show him! She would just go to Texas and show him that he was wrong about her. She searched her mind for everything that Jarratt had told her about his home. Thirty-five miles outside of Pecos was about all that he had said, but she could use a map to get to Pecos and get directions to his ranch there. *Let's see, most of my clothes won't do. I'll need jeans and boots and*

97

a western shirt or two. I'll pack some books and magazines for entertainment when I'm not keeping house. She reached out and picked up the telephone, dialing the hotel's casino.

The graveyard pit boss answered the phone.

"Tommy? This is Cassandra Howard. Leave a note for Joe to arrange a leave of absence for me as soon as possible. Of course without pay. No, Tommy, I'm not pregnant. Thanks."

Texas, here I come, Cassandra thought as she hauled down her suitcases out of the closet and dusted them off. She reached up and felt the diamond heart that was still around her neck, then very deliberately reached up and took it off. Jarratt had given her the necklace as a good-bye gift. *I'm not going to wear it,* Cassandra thought, *because I'll be damned if it's going to be good-bye.*

CHAPTER SIX

I have never seen so much dust in all my life, Cassandra thought to herself as she gingerly eased the Firebird down the rutted gravel road that led to Jarratt's ranch house. Although Las Vegas was desert, for some reason it certainly did not seem this dusty! A cool October wind blew across the rolling hills of west Texas, stirring the desolate little scrub brush and howling around her car. *This is not much more than a desert,* she thought. The dry rolling land, dotted with scrubby plants and bushes was covered with just enough grass to allow some grazing. Cassandra sat forward to ease the ache in her back and sincerely hoped that she would reach the ranch house before too much longer. She had been driving for three days, spending the better part of the day on the road and sleeping in dingy motels at night, and she was tired. She had spent the last night in El Paso, where she had ducked across the border for a little shopping, and had left early this morning for Pecos. It was now the middle of the afternoon, and she longed to get out of the car and have a warm shower.

As Cassandra drew nearer and nearer Jarratt's home, both her excitement and her apprehension grew. She would be seeing Jarratt again! That was enough to make her want to cry for joy. In the last month she had missed him unbearably, dreaming of him every night, thinking of him every day. Cassandra had not been able to get away from Las Vegas as quickly as she had hoped when she had made up her mind to come to Texas. First the casino had insisted that she work the month, then Sharon had come home from the hospital and Cassandra had helped her and her parents make arrangements for her to move back to Missouri. But finally she had left her job and closed up her condominium and set out for Texas and Jarratt.

But would Jarratt be glad to see her, or would he be angry with her for coming? Although he seemed very easygoing on the surface, Cassandra suspected that he had a will of steel, and that once he had made up his mind, he would be very unlikely to change it. Well, so did she, and when she showed him how she could adjust to his life-style, he wouldn't have any choice but to change his attitude, she thought confidently. She shivered a little in spite of the heater in the car, hoping that her optimism was warranted.

As she rounded a bend in the road, an old Victorian house came into view from behind a low hill, surrounded by a number of smaller buildings. *So I've arrived,* she thought with relief, glad that the laconic old rancher in Pecos had known what he was talking about when he gave her directions to this place. The old house was magnificent, gleaming white in the bright sun. It was three stories high, with a little tower on one side and bright stained glass windows winking in the sunlight. A wide porch ran around the front of the house and appeared to go all the way around the lower story, although Cassandra knew that the porch probably stopped in the back. As she drove closer, she could pick out a huge barn behind the house and what looked like a bunkhouse. The corral to one side of the barn had several horses in it, and in the distance she could see cattle grazing. *So this is it,* she thought. *Jarratt's home. No wonder he doesn't want to leave,* she thought. *This is beautiful.*

As Cassandra pulled up in front of the house she looked around for a sign of life. The horses in the corral had noticed her arrival and were snorting and pawing the ground, but so far no one seemed aware of her arrival. Grabbing the smaller of her two suitcases from the trunk, she marched up to the front door, biting her lip as a sudden attack of nerves left her weak. She wanted to turn around and drive straight back to Las Vegas! No, she hadn't come this far to back out now. Not finding a door-bell, she knocked on the door and waited a moment, then knocked again. It would be just her luck if no one was here and she had to wait hours on the front doorstep.

Just as Cassandra was about to give up, the door creaked open and a thin, wizened old woman stuck her face out. She looked at Cassandra suspiciously. "What can I do for you?" she asked warily.

"You must be Martha," Cassandra said as she put on her brightest smile. "I'm Cassandra Howard from Las Vegas. Jarratt told me so much about you." Martha said nothing as Cassandra drew her sweater more tightly around her body. "Didn't he mention that I'm expected?" Cassandra lied earnestly.

"No, Jarratt didn't mention nothin' about no company," Martha said firmly as she prepared to shut the door.

"Then I'm sure that it just slipped his mind," Cassandra replied smoothly as she reached for the screen door and opened it. Martha could not very well shut the door in her face now. "I'd like to come in," she said innocently. "It's cold out here and I've been driving for three days."

"But Jarratt didn't say nothin' about you comin'," Martha repeated suspiciously.

The poker face that Cassandra had learned to maintain in the casinos served her well now. "Do you really think I would drive this far if I hadn't been invited?" she asked reasonably.

Martha wavered for a moment. "Guess not," she acknowledged. She threw open the door and took Cassandra's suitcase from her. "This all you brought?" she asked.

"No, my other suitcase is in the car," Cassandra replied.

"Well, if it's any heavier than this one I can't carry it," Martha admitted grudgingly as she carried the smaller suitcase into what Cassandra thought must have once been the parlor and was now a living room. "If you'll go get it, I'll show you where to put them. I ain't got no help today."

"Of course," Cassandra replied as she scurried out of the house and brought in her other suitcase. Martha had disappeared when she returned to the parlor, and Cassandra looked around the front rooms with interest. The furnishings were a hodgepodge of styles, with everything from old Victorian family pieces to fifties traditional, yet the overall effect was pleasing. Faded prints covered equally faded wallpaper, and Cassandra thought that with a little judicious weeding of the furniture and a woman's touch with the accessories, the house could be quite lovely.

Martha returned and thrust a steaming cup of coffee into Cassandra's hands. "Here, this'll warm you up some," the old woman said grudgingly. She looked Cassandra over, taking in her rumpled but expensive purple slacks and matching sweater as Cassandra tried to swallow the thick, bitter coffee. "You one of those fancy women?" Martha asked suddenly.

"No," Cassandra replied, angry and embarrassed at the same time. Martha took a step backward at the vehemence in Cassandra's tone. Cassandra took pity on the woman and softened her voice somewhat. "I'm a dealer," she added. "In a casino."

Martha's eyes widened but she said nothing. Cassandra finished as much of the coffee as she could and handed the cup back to Martha, then reached down and picked up both suitcases. "If you'll show me where to put these?" she asked.

Martha led Cassandra to the back of the house and up the flight of stairs to the second floor. Cassandra noticed that the flight stopped here and that there didn't appear to be a way into the third story. "How can you get up to the third floor?" she asked Martha.

Martha looked at Cassandra in disbelief. "That's the attic," she said shortly. "Only an idiot would want to go up there." Suitably chastened, Cassandra followed Martha to the end of a corridor and opened the door to what turned out to be a charming bedroom, still furnished and decorated with the original Victorian furniture. The old iron bed had an elaborately wrought headboard and footboard, and the golden oak dresser and writing table shone with a mellow glow. Next to the bed an old washstand served as a night table.

"This is lovely, Martha," Cassandra breathed. "Thank you for showing me up."

"Dinner's at six," the old woman replied.

"I'll be down before then to help you get it on the table," Cassandra assured the old woman, who looked at her disbelievingly and walked out of the room.

Cassandra found a bathroom at the end of the hall. It did not have a shower, but the old claw-footed bathtub was quite large, and Cassandra drew a bath and gratefully removed the grime from her body, bending herself into a pretzel shape to wash her hair under the tap. She found clean towels in the cupboard and dried swiftly in the cold bathroom, then pulled on the clean underwear and new jeans and shirt that she had purchased in Las Vegas. When would Jarratt get back to the ranch? she wondered. It was already late in the afternoon. She had not asked Martha earlier, and she didn't want to seek the old woman out and ask her right now. She applied her makeup and was blowing her hair dry when she heard the sound of a large vehicle driving slowly over the rutted road. She looked out the window and saw a huge maroon pickup towing a matching trailer with three cattle in it. The pickup pulled up beside her Firebird and Jarratt hopped out of the cab, looked at the Firebird in disbelief, then said something to the passengers in the truck and ran for the front door. One of the men scooted over and drove the pickup toward the barn.

The front door banged shut, and Cassandra could hear the sound of Jarratt's footsteps as they echoed through the house. She could hear him clomping throughout the lower floor, then she heard his footsteps on the stairs, bolting up them two at a time. Cassandra sat quietly on the bed, fixing a calm smile to her face, suddenly horribly apprehensive but not wanting Jarratt to know that. He threw open the door and looked at Cassandra with a mixture of anger and incredulity. "What the hell are you doing here?" he demanded.

"Hello, Jarratt," Cassandra replied calmly as she quickly and carefully masked her amazement at the Jarratt Vandenburg that stood in front of her. In Las Vegas he had always seemed so cultured, so polished, so *clean*. This Jarratt was covered from head to toe with dust and brown spatters of mud. A layer of dirt coated the seat of his pants and thick chunks of mud covered what must have been the oldest, most run-down work boots in Texas. A sweat-ringed hat sat back on his head. Even his dark hair was covered with a coating of dust, and from his direction a peculiar odor wafted across the room. Cassandra wrinkled her nose and sniffed the air. "What's that funny smell?" she asked.

"Manure," Jarratt replied heavily. "That's cow sh—"

"I know what manure is," Cassandra broke in quickly.

"You didn't answer my question," Jarratt said firmly. "How did you persuade Martha to let you in?"

"I lied," Cassandra replied calmly.

"Cassandra, I don't want you here. I suggest that you pack your bags and get yourself right back to Las Vegas," Jarratt replied. His anger was fading, however, to be replaced with something resembling indifference.

"No way," Cassandra replied, sitting cross-legged on the bed and staring at Jarratt impudently. "I have something to do first."

"Just what do you think you have to do out here?" Jarratt asked boredly.

"Prove you wrong," Cassandra replied, not wasting any time on verbal fencing. Puzzled by Jarratt's attitude, she pulled a brush through her hair slowly as she talked. "You're so damn sure that we can't make it here, I've come to show you that we can. I took a leave of absence from the casino and I'm going to stay here with you, in this house, for as long as it takes to get it through your hard head that I'll be all right here. You don't want to gamble on our future? All right, we won't. I'll show you that there will be no gamble involved."

"My, my, aren't you sure of yourself," Jarratt replied mockingly. "What will you do if I just throw you out?"

"Oh, you won't do that," Cassandra replied softly. "You love me too much to do that."

Jarratt flinched, but his face remained a cool mask. "No, I won't throw you out, Cassandra, but neither will I play host to you. I'm in the middle of worming, and I've got to gather up all the cattle I'm going to sell and get them to market before I have to start winter feeding, so I'll be gone most of the time. If you want to stay under those conditions, fine."

"That's all right, Jarratt," Cassandra said, assuming a

confidence that she suddenly no longer felt. "It will be that way after we're married."

"Fine. Supper's at six," he replied as he stepped to the door. "See you then." Jarratt stepped out and closed the door behind him, leaving Cassandra staring in wonder at his retreating form. Although she had not expected him to be glad to see her, far from that, she certainly had not expected this cool, detached welcome. Anger, maybe, and perhaps a more enthusiastic attempt to force her to go, but not an unconcerned "Fine, supper's at six" when she refused to leave. Unless he was not attracted to her anymore. What if it had been just a fling for him! What if he really didn't care for her! Cassandra paced the floor for a few minutes, then shrugged her shoulders and perched on the edge of the bed. Well, she had come, and only by staying would she find out if Jarratt no longer cared for her, or if he was putting up a front.

Cassandra checked her watch and bounced off the bed. It was after five already, and she had promised to help Martha. She wandered downstairs and followed her nose to the huge old kitchen located in the back of the house. Jarratt was nowhere to be seen, but Martha was bent over the counter cutting up a chicken, her face puckered into a frown of concentration. She looked up as Cassandra entered the room, scowling at the interruption. "What do you need?" she asked Cassandra.

"I said I'd help you with supper," Cassandra reminded the woman. "What can I do to help?"

Martha's face softened a little. "Well, I need to tend to this cake I made this afternoon," she said. "If you'll cut up this chicken, I can do that."

"Of course," Cassandra replied, swallowing hard. She had never cut up a chicken in her life, preferring to buy the precut pieces from the grocery. But surely it wasn't that hard, she told herself as she approached the half cut-up chicken. It was well on the way to dismemberment, but the other two on the counter were still whole. Cassandra looked at the chicken warily, then shrugged her shoulders and picked up the knife. Not knowing where to begin, she hacked off the bottom third of the wing, then very carefully cut both wings into three pieces. She laid those on the counter, then proceeded to cut up the rest of the chicken the best that she could. She put those pieces in a large plastic bowl and picked up one of the uncut chickens.

Now what? she thought as she very carefully took apart the wings as she had on the other chicken. Oh, well, at least the knife was sharp. Cassandra whittled away merrily, occasionally encountering bone when she wasn't expecting to, but if she could not cut the bones, she could always break them. She finished both chickens and turned to Martha, who was still absorbed in icing her cake. "What do you want me to do with the chicken?" she asked.

"Fry it," Martha replied. "The grease is just above the stove in the coffee can. Flour's above the sink."

At least she was on familiar territory there, Cassandra thought as she dredged the chicken and plopped it into the hot grease. One of the few things that her mother had managed to teach her to cook was fried chicken. Only after the chicken was in the grease did Cassandra remember that she had not salted it. Oops! Oh, well, she could fix that. She grabbed the salt shaker and liberally dusted the chicken in the pan with salt. Martha had finished the cake and was opening a home-canned jar of beans into a large pot. "How's the chicken coming?" she asked as she carried the heavy pot to the stove.

"Just fine," Cassandra assured her.

"Good. I'll keep an eye on it if you'll set the table," Martha said as she lifted the lid and looked down at the bubbling chicken. "What in the world?" she asked, looking at Cassandra as though Cassandra had wandered off a flying saucer.

"What did you say, Martha?" Cassandra asked, her back to Martha.

"Nothin,'" the old woman replied, shaking her head.

As instructed, Cassandra set six places at the table. Jarratt had two men, both bachelors, who worked for him full-time and who ate at the house, although they lived down at the bunkhouse. Martha's husband also worked for Jarratt, and although he and Martha shared a small house of their own behind the bunkhouse, they too ate at the main house. Martha let Cassandra make up a huge pitcher of iced tea and pour it into glasses. Promptly at six Jarratt, freshly showered and shaved, walked through the door from the main part of the house as three clean men came through the back door. Jarratt's eyes widened at the sight of Cassandra calmly pouring tea into the last glass, but his indifferent mask fell back into place almost immediately. The other three men's eyes widened at the sight of the pretty stranger wearing obviously brand-new western clothes. Not waiting for an introduction from Jarratt, she walked up to the youngest of them and extended her hand. "I'm Cassandra Howard from Las Vegas," she said, flashing her best smile. "I'm Jarratt's houseguest." She winked at Jarratt impudently, daring him to contradict her.

The freckle-faced young man, who had been in the pickup and who had heard Jarratt's string of expletives on spotting the Firebird, looked from Jarratt to Cassandra wonderingly, but was quickly captivated by Cassandra's smile. "I'm B. C. Thompkins," he drawled. "I'm mightly glad to meet you!"

"Thank you," Cassandra replied sincerely. She turned

to the older of the two men who had come in with B.C. "And you're Pete?" she asked. "Martha's husband?"

Unlike B.C., Pete was reserving judgment on Cassandra. He shook her hand formally. "Hello," he said simply.

"And I'm Dusty Rogers," the third man said as he introduced himself to her, shaking her hand firmly. Small, gray-haired, and tough-looking, he could have been anywhere between forty and sixty. He looked at her and Jarratt appraisingly, then pulled out a chair from the table and sat down. "Martha, where's that chicken? I'm starving!"

The other men took their places at the table while Cassandra and Martha put huge bowls and platters of food before the men. *We'll never be able to eat all this,* Cassandra thought as she sat down in the nearest empty chair, between B.C. and Dusty. Martha sat down last and Jarratt picked up the platter of chicken. "What the hell . . ." he mouthed as he speared a piece of the chicken on the serving fork.

The men's eyes widened as the chicken platter was passed around the table. They all took several of the pieces in silence, looking at Martha strangely as they did so. They passed around the fresh-baked cornbread, three vegetables, and the huge salad. Cassandra stared in astonishment at the sheer quantity of food that Jarratt and the men put on their plates. Jarratt picked up a piece of the chicken and bit in. He chewed it thoughtfully but said nothing.

Pete picked up a piece of the chicken and looked at it strangely. "Don't look like any piece of chicken I ever seen before," he commented sagely to his wife, who snorted audibly.

Jarratt looked from Martha to Cassandra as a light dawned in his eyes. "I'll bet this is a Las Vegas chicken," he commented dryly.

Five sets of eyes turned on Cassandra. She blushed furiously, knowing that the chicken had not been cut up properly, and probably had not been cooked properly, and that she could not let Martha take credit for this fiasco, even though Jarratt's men would probably think she was an idiot. Determined to make the best of the situation, she flashed an engaging grin. "That's right," she said brightly. "It's a Las Vegas chicken, all right. The one that didn't get away." Ignoring the others, she looked Jarratt in the eye and was gratified to see a blush creep up his face.

"Well, I think it's good," B.C. said brightly as he finished off his first piece in one bite.

Nothing more was said as the men finished the main dish and waited for Martha to serve the frosted cake she had made for dessert.

It really wasn't too bad, Cassandra thought later, remembering B.C.'s remark as she helped Martha clean off the table and load the dishwasher. Everyone had eaten the chicken. It had just been a little too salty in a few places, and the pieces had been peculiar, but that was all, so maybe they didn't think she was too stupid. Cassandra looked at her watch as she and Martha loaded the last of the dishes. It was barely seven in the evening. She still would have been at the casino in Vegas, and she was sure that everyone wouldn't be going to bed at this early hour. What would they do to pass the time tonight?

Cassandra wandered out to the living room and peeked inside. Jarratt was nowhere to be seen, but the three men were lined up in front of the television set, using the remote control dial to flip through the channels. When they saw her at the door they motioned her inside and made room for her to sit on the couch. "The TV in the bunkhouse is broke," B.C. volunteered cheerfully. "And Pete's too cheap to buy one for Martha." This was met by loud guffaws from Dusty.

110

"No sense in buying one when we can watch this one for free," Pete replied laconically.

"Well, is there anything on tonight?" Cassandra asked brightly.

"Don't matter if there is or there isn't," Dusty replied indifferently. "We'll watch it anyway. Ain't nothin' else to do."

"Oh, I don't know," Cassandra said slowly. "Any of you guys have a pack of cards?"

"Cards?" B.C. asked.

"Sure, cards," Cassandra said enthusiastically. "That would beat a dull TV show."

"Only game we play is poker," Pete spoke up. "Don't know any ladylike games."

"Poker will be fine," Cassandra nodded, hiding her smile.

B.C. headed toward the bunkhouse while Dusty and Cassandra removed the tablecloth from the large, seldom-used dining room table. B.C. returned with a pack of cards and a box of chips and Pete solemnly shuffled the cards and dealt.

"What kind of stakes?" Cassandra asked innocently.

"Dollar limit," Pete replied. "We play real poker here, no penny ante stuff." Cassandra smothered a giggle, thinking of the hundreds of thousands of dollars she had seen bet in Las Vegas.

Cassandra picked up her cards and her unerring instinct took over, aided of course by her years as a dealer. She immediately won three hands in a row, laughing as the men teased her about beginner's luck. Then play began in earnest. They played hard, and they played silently, and Cassandra had to admit that these men were extremely skilled at the game. As the pile of chips grew slowly larger and larger in front of her, the men's expressions went from

111

condescension to amusement to outright amazement. The woman could play poker like a pro!

Time flew for Cassandra as it never had in the casino. Playing against these men was a real challenge, she acknowledged as Dusty won a hand and she had to pay up. This was fun! As they played hand after hand Cassandra continued to win consistently, yet she lost often enough to make the game interesting. As she shuffled and dealt the cards for the umpteenth time, B.C. looked at her hands in wonder. "You shuffle like a pro," he said marvelingly.

"I am a pro," Cassandra replied calmly. "I deal in Las Vegas for a living." She held her breath, hoping that none of the men would feel that she had hustled them.

"No kidding," B.C. breathed in wonder. "I thought you were a dancer or something."

"Well, I'll be damned," Dusty laughed, slapping his knee with his palm. "A dealer! Well, no wonder you play like you do!"

"Good game," Pete said simply, although there was a distinct gleam of admiration in his eyes as he said it.

"You guys play a mighty good game too," Cassandra told them warmly. "You're better than some players, Dusty."

"What's a player?" Dusty asked.

Cassandra told them, then B.C. and Dusty plied her with questions about Las Vegas for another hour, and even Pete had a question or two. Their game forgotten, Cassandra entertained them with stories of her life in Las Vegas. As they were all laughing as hard as they could at her story about the millionaire's poodle who got loose in the casino, Jarratt walked by the dining room and wandered in, curious.

"Too bad you had paperwork tonight. Boy, you ought to see this girl play poker!" B.C. said to Jarratt with admiration.

112

"I've seen her play," Jarratt replied dryly.

"As far as I'm concerned, she can play with me anytime," B.C. enthused. Jarratt's eyes narrowed but he said nothing.

"She's all right, Jarratt," Dusty said quietly.

Pleased that she had redeemed herself in the ranch hands' eyes, Cassandra gathered up the cards and stacked them neatly. "For next time," she said. The men got out their wallets and started digging out money. Jarratt's eyes flickered with anger and Cassandra protested. "Please, no," she said. "You didn't know I was a pro."

"A bet's a bet," Pete replied as he handed her some bills. B.C. handed her a five and a ten.

"It was worth it to get to see you play," Dusty replied as he handed her a ten. "Sometime could you give me some pointers?"

"Of course," Cassandra replied warmly as she took the money.

The men bade her good night and trooped out, leaving her and Jarratt standing alone in the middle of the dining room. The air between them crackled with tension.

Jarratt's mouth lifted a little at the edges. "So you've made three conquests already," he said sardonically. "I wondered if you ever would, after that chicken."

Cassandra shrugged. "They're very nice," she said. "And damn good poker players." She hesitated, biting her lip. "I'm sorry I won their money though."

"Don't be," Jarratt replied indifferently. "For what I pay them they can afford it."

Cassandra looked at his impassive face. His reaction was much too cool, too controlled, and it bothered her, yet she didn't know what to do about it. Looking at her watch, she gasped. "I didn't realize it was so late," she said. "I think I'll go on up to bed." She turned to him and smiled at him provocatively, knowing that in Las Vegas her come-hither look had turned Jarratt to jelly.

"I've asked Martha and Pete to stay here in the house with us as long as you're here," Jarratt volunteered casually, showing no visible response to her sensual smile.

Cassandra started. "And why do that? We're grown-ups. And we're well past the point in our relationship of needing a chaperone," she added sardonically.

"You're not in Las Vegas now," Jarratt replied heavily. "Attitudes are a little different here in west Texas, Cassandra. People do notice that kind of thing and don't particularly appreciate it."

"Oh, goodness, and we wouldn't want to ruin poor little Jarratt's reputation, now would we?" Cassandra cooed sarcastically, only the glitter in her eyes betraying her true anger. She reached up and patted Jarratt's jaw softly, laughing a little when he flinched away. "What's the matter, Jarratt?" she taunted. "Afraid I'll seduce you?"

A telltale wave of color ran up Jarratt's face. "I'll be sleeping on the divan in the study," he said stiffly. "Martha and Pete will be in my room."

"Oh, the one right next to mine," Cassandra taunted him, remembering the big bedroom decorated in bright shades of blue and gold. "Well, you can tell Martha that I only sleepwalk every other night. I won't be bothering her or you." She turned on her heel and left Jarratt standing in the middle of the dining room.

Damn, damn, damn, Cassandra thought as she stripped off her clothes and climbed into bed. She thought a minute, then climbed out of bed and opened her suitcase. *I guess I better wear a gown,* she thought sardonically. *After all, this is Texas,* she reminded herself as she pulled the gown over her head. Yes, Cassandra admitted to herself, she had been counting on seducing Jarratt, tantalizing him, capturing him with the great physical rapport that

114

they shared. Unfortunately he had seen through her, and was using Pete and Martha as a smokescreen, a further barrier between them. *I wonder what would happen if I went down there anyway,* Cassandra asked herself, opening the door, but the thought of Martha's wrinkled old face stopped her in her tracks. No, if she was going to win this one, she was going to need Martha on her side, and getting caught in Jarratt's bed was not the way to manage that! She would accomplish nothing by offending the sensibilities of Jarratt's friends.

But, on the other hand, Jarratt must still be attracted to me, Cassandra reminded herself as she pulled the covers over her body and turned out the light. *Otherwise why would he even bother to ask Martha and Pete to stay? Yes, he still loves me,* Cassandra thought as she grinned wickedly into the dark room. *He doesn't even trust himself alone with me! Okay, so I can't use sex on you, Jarratt. But I have other weapons, man, that you never even thought about!*

CHAPTER SEVEN

Cassandra leaned over the fence and peered with interest at the mooing, pawing herd of cattle that Jarratt and his men were driving into the pen. It had been three days since she had arrived at the ranch, and these were the first cattle that she had seen apart from those that had been in the pickup the day she had arrived. Apparently Jarratt's ranch was huge, and the cattle were sparsely scattered over the many acres of land.

Cassandra's face softened as she watched Jarratt, astride a large brown gelding, as he and the skilled horse worked the cattle into the small pen. The muscles rippled in his bare arms as he and the horse moved in graceful harmony, dodging, driving, and coaxing the reluctant animals through the small gate. B.C. had told her this morning that they would be worming these cattle today, and that this would be a good chance to see some real ranch work up close.

Pete and Dusty were in the corral with the cattle, forcing one at a time through what Cassandra had heard Jarratt call a "chute." There B.C. was giving each of them a shot in the neck with a large syringe that was mounted on a pistol grip. He leaned over the chute and expertly jabbed the huge needle into the thick hide of the neck, sometimes having to dodge as an angry cow turned on him and tried to butt him with her head. B.C. then opened the chute and let the cow into a second pen, from which they would either be taken back to pasture or sent to market. It was late in the morning and the men had been at this since dawn, but Dusty had said earlier that they were making good time and would be finished earlier than expected.

Cassandra hopped off the fence and trotted toward the house. She washed her dirty hands at the outside tap, shivering a little when the cold water hit her fingers, then dried her hands with a rag left hanging on the faucet for that purpose. In the kitchen she washed her hands again, this time with soap, and peeked into the stove. Martha had put on a roast right after breakfast, and it had turned an enticing shade of crusty brown. Cassandra shut the oven and began setting the table.

Martha wandered in with a load of clean dishtowels. "Get your fill of worming?" she asked with the slightest glimmer of amusement in her wrinkled little face.

"I can see why women's lib has never been that big in west Texas," Cassandra admitted wryly. "I'd be willing to leave that kind of work to the men. Although," she added thoughtfully, "I'll bet there's many a wife and daughter on a smaller ranch who has to get out and do that kind of thing."

"Yes, there are," Martha acknowledged frankly. "Would you mind making the tea?"

Cassandra nodded and got out the pitcher. Although Martha had not let her near the stove again, she had willingly accepted Cassandra's help with setting the table and making the tea, and she had acted grudgingly grateful when Cassandra had volunteered to clean up the kitchen for the last two nights. Although the old woman was still reserving judgment on the Las Vegas stranger, it was obvious that she hadn't been expecting Cassandra to help with the chores.

117

Jarratt and the men trooped in just as Martha and Cassandra put the last of the food on the table. They had washed up outside, but their clothes were still dusty and they carried that peculiar odor that Cassandra had learned to identify as "cow." Now that the men had gotten used to her presence, they talked freely to her and with each other, perhaps curbing the ribaldry for her and Martha's benefit, but nevertheless displaying plenty of keen humor. Jarratt joined in the fun, and he had even made a few funny comments to Cassandra. He had not approached her since they had talked in the dining room after the poker game, but Cassandra had caught him staring at her a few times with a peculiar expression on his face that she simply could not understand. How does he feel about having me here now? she wondered as she ate the last of her roast. With Jarratt, she simply could not tell.

The meal finished, Cassandra and Martha cleared the table and loaded the diswasher. As Martha put in the last plate, she hesitated, then spoke to Cassandra gruffly. "You don't have to clean the upstairs every morning," she said. "I know you been scrubbing out that bathtub and sweeping the floors. You're company."

Cassandra shook her head and smiled a little. "It's all right, Martha," she said softly. "I use the bathroom and track up the floor, don't I?"

Martha looked at Cassandra and shrugged her shoulders and shut the dishwasher. "Well, I can't stop you," she said as she pushed the button. Cassandra watched Martha as she shuffled out of the room, wondering if she had offended the woman by helping.

Cassandra headed for the back door, opening the screen door onto the porch and smashing it right into Jarratt, who grunted and swore softly. "Can't you look through the screen?" he demanded, nursing his banged elbow.

"Sorry," Cassandra muttered, contrite. First Martha,

now Jarratt! She couldn't please anybody today. She slid past him and pushed open the outer door.

"Cassandra," Jarratt called softly.

"Yes?" she asked.

"That was Martha's way of thanking you," he said softly.

"You heard?" Cassandra asked.

Jarratt nodded. "She appreciates the help, and so do I," he said as he walked into the house.

Shaking her head, Cassandra headed back toward the corral and leaned against the fence, watching as Dusty and Pete vaccinated the rest of the cattle. As they drove the needle into the neck of the last cow, B.C. came and stood beside Cassandra. "Well, what do you think?" he asked her shyly.

"I think you guys work hard," she replied honestly.

B.C. shrugged. "It's a living until I can get my own spread," he replied.

Cassandra watched the pen full of cattle with interest. The cattle all appeared to be of the same breed, although there were a variety of sizes and genders. She observed the milling herd for a few minutes in puzzlement, then asked the first question that popped into her head. "How do you tell a cow from a bull?" she asked innocently.

B.C. turned a bright shade of crimson. "Well, you look at them, ma'am," he stammered.

Cassandra looked at the various cattle with bewilderment. "They don't look that much different to me," she admitted with confusion.

B.C. turned even redder. "Cows have a bag, and bulls, well, bulls have—have one of those," he explained as one of the young bulls walked by.

Cassandra blushed to the roots of her hair. "Oh," she said simply.

"And that one's a steer," Dusty volunteered as he pointed out yet another animal. "He's had brain surgery. We altered his whole outlook on life."

"Cute, Dusty," Cassandra replied, blushing again.

"Well, we're through for the day, B.C., as soon as Pete lets those cattle back out of the pen. What do you say we saddle up and go for a ride?"

B.C. nodded eagerly. Cassandra had learned that very little of a cowboy's work was done from the back of a horse, and that the modern cowboy tended to view riding as a pleasure rather than as a duty. Dusty turned to Cassandra and smiled. "Like to come?"

"I'd love to," she replied wistfully, "but I've never been on the back of a horse in my life."

B.C.'s face fell, but Dusty looked at her thoughtfully. "Scared?" he asked.

"Of course not!" Cassandra replied indignantly. "I've just never had the opportunity to learn."

"Do you want to learn?" B.C. asked eagerly. "We can teach you."

Cassandra thought about the big horses that she had seen on her first day at the ranch. She had honestly never thought much about riding a horse, but why not? It didn't look that hard. And besides, if she was going to stay here for the rest of her life, she had better learn. "Sounds good," she said. "I'd love to, in fact."

The three of them wandered into the barn and Dusty and B.C. saddled their own horses. They then selected a small gray mare that seemed gentle, and led the three animals out of the barn. "No, Cassandra, you mount from the left," Dusty instructed her when she approached the wrong side of the horse. Obediently she walked around the mare and extended her booted foot. The mare flinched and skitted a little.

"Come on, horse," Dusty said as he held the reins for Cassandra. This time Cassandra was able to get her foot into the stirrup and swing her leg over the back of the horse, just like in the movies. Almost immediately the horse reared up, throwing Cassandra over backward into a small patch of grass. She lay back, winded, as the sky swirled around above her.

"Cassandra! Are you all right?" B.C. demanded as Dusty let loose with a stream of foul words in the horse's direction.

Cassandra pushed herself up groggily, sitting quietly as the sky gradually became still. "Yes, I'm fine," she replied softly.

"What the hell's going on?" Jarratt called as he ran out the back door, banging it behind him, and knelt beside Cassandra. "Are you all right?" he demanded with real worry in his voice.

"Your horse doesn't like me," Cassandra replied wryly, flexing her back and checking her arms and legs. One minor scratch. She had gotten off light.

"Jewel got spooked yesterday by a rattlesnake," Jarratt informed Dusty and B.C. angrily. "You should have never put a novice up on her today."

"Sorry, Jarratt," B.C. mumbled.

"Come on, Cassandra," Jarratt replied heavily. "I'll take you back to the house."

"No, Jarratt." She grinned at B.C. and Dusty. "Do you have another horse I could ride?"

"Now, Cassandra," Jarratt began.

Cassandra rounded on him spiritedly. "Do you want me to be scared for the rest of my life?" she demanded. Her face softened. "I'd really like to learn."

Jarratt shrugged. "Saddle Samson for her," he ordered Dusty. "I'll ride this one." He mounted the little horse and let her rear up a few times, then dug his heels into her sides and galloped away.

Dusty and B.C. stared after Jarratt with a look of astonishment on their faces. "What's wrong?" Cassandra asked them anxiously.

"Samson is his favorite horse," Dusty replied. "Usually he doesn't let anyone else ride him."

B.C. saddled the big gelding that Jarratt had ridden earlier in the day, and although they had to help Cassandra onto the horse, Samson proved to be a gentle animal. As they walked and trotted the horses across the pasture Dusty explained that Jarratt, and most other riders, usually rode a gentle, easily handled horse in preference to the "spirited stallions" that populated books. B.C. and Dusty demonstrated how to stand in the saddle when trotting or galloping and let Cassandra practice a little, then they rode through the sparse pasture, making allowances for Cassandra's inexperience but nevertheless showing her a small part of the Vandenburg ranch. Although the landscape was bleak, Cassandra was beginning to appreciate the land as a peculiarly beautiful place, not one that would appeal to everybody, but one that had a definite attraction to a tough, independent sort of person like Jarratt, she thought. And me.

They rode for three hours, then Cassandra took a long hot bath, hoping to prevent herself from becoming sore. Nevertheless, she was moving stiffly when she came down to help Martha with supper, and made no effort to organize an evening poker game. She was just too sore to sit in a hard chair. Instead, she sat on the soft couch and watched television with Pete and Martha and was genuinely surprised at how terrible most of the prime-time programs were. In Las Vegas she had been either coming on or going off a shift during those hours, and she hadn't watched television in years. She suffered through two programs, then found a sweater and walked stiffly to the front porch, where she shut the door behind her and leaned against one of the posts, staring up at the stars. There was no moon out, and the stars spangled the sky even more brightly here than on Mount Charleston. Breathing in the cool clean air, Cassandra stared into the night sky, remembering the night on Mount Charleston with a wistful longing for a return to the way things had been between her and Jarratt in Las Vegas.

"What's the matter, can't sit down?" a deep voice whispered at her elbow.

"Only on something *very* soft," Cassandra admitted as warm shivers trickled down her spine. Jarratt was so close to her that she could feel his warm breath in her hair.

"Did you enjoy your ride?" Jarratt asked as he moved away and leaned on the opposite post.

"Yes, I did," Cassandra replied. "The ranch is beautiful."

Jarratt shrugged. "I guess it depends on your taste," he said indifferently.

"Well, I like it," Cassandra replied firmly. "When do you take your cattle to market?" she asked quickly, determined to change the subject before they got into another argument.

"Sometime next week," Jarratt replied. "Then we feed all winter."

"Never stops, does it?" Cassandra observed.

"Never," Jarratt admitted. Cassandra moved away from the post and winced as a spasm of pain caught her. "You're sore," Jarratt accused her softly. "I knew you would be sore from the fall."

"I'm not sore from the fall," Cassandra replied quickly. "At least I'm not sore there from the fall," she amended sheepishly. "We rode for three hours."

"Oh, good grief," Jarratt complained. "Didn't any of you lamebrains have any common sense at all? You shouldn't have ridden for three hours if you're not used to riding!"

Cassandra shrugged. "I enjoyed it," she replied.

"Well, have Martha give you some liniment to put on it," Jarratt replied. "Good night, Annie Oakley."

" 'Night, Wild Bill," Cassandra replied softly. *He was almost friendly,* Cassandra thought as she watched Jarratt walk through the door. *Maybe I'm reaching him, after all,* she thought.

Cassandra was sore for a day or two, but she recovered quickly and by the time she had been at the ranch for three weeks she had become an adequate if not accomplished rider. Dusty and B.C. took her out every time they went, and after she had become fairly secure and confident in the saddle, she would take out one of the horses herself and ride around the ranch a little, always staying in view of the house. She had no illusions about being an experienced country girl, and she had no desire to ride off and get herself lost. Once over her spooking, Jewel proved to be an excellent mount for Cassandra, and she spent many happy hours on the little horse.

Cassandra insisted on doing her share of the housework, much to Martha's continued amazement. Not one to talk, the little old woman would thank her gruffly sometimes, but Cassandra noticed that Martha was trusting her more around the stove, and had even let Cassandra cook supper by herself one evening when Martha and Pete needed to drive into Pecos. Cassandra had broiled steaks and baked potatoes that night, but she managed to get the meal on the table without burning or undercooking any of it. Jarratt thanked her for the meal along with the other men, acting a little surprised at her accomplishment. Cassandra had winked impudently at him in front of B.C. and Dusty had commented that the gamble he refused to take was becoming less of a gamble every day, to which Jarratt

124

had grunted and left the room. *But he's coming around,* she told herself. *I'm making him come around.*

Jarratt had become quite friendly to Cassandra in fact. He had offered to let her drive with him to the cattle auction in Pecos, and Cassandra had watched the process of auctioning off hundreds of cows at a time in amazement. The auctioneer, a ruddy middle-aged man with a speedy tongue, auctioned off one cow or bull or steer at a time, or maybe he sold a cow with her calf. The animals, carefully numbered, were run before the customers and bidding began. The bidding was so fast that Cassandra literally could not understand the words, but at some point, usually thirty to forty-five seconds after the auctioneer had begun, he would stop and clearly announce who had bought the animal and the price per pound for which it had sold. Then it would begin again. Jarratt had stayed until all of his animals had been sold, then he collected his hefty checks in the office before he left. They spent the better part of the day at the auction, after which Jarratt treated her to dinner at the restaurant in Pecos. The food had been plain but substantial, and Cassandra had enjoyed the day thoroughly, only becoming a little disappointed when Jarratt bade her good night at the door. But he was beginning to talk to her freely, openly, the way that he had in Las Vegas, and Cassandra knew that she could count on the day, coming soon, when she would wear down Jarratt's resistance and he would decide that he could marry her after all.

But during the month she had been here, Cassandra could detect a change within herself, a change that frightened her, a change that could tear her world apart. It started simply at first. She would be as happy as a lark all morning, cleaning, or riding, or cooking with Martha, but by the middle of the afternoon she would be wandering around the house, waiting for suppertime, or wandering out to the barn to talk to the horses or maybe go for another short ride. Soon she was wandering around all afternoon, looking for something with which to fill the time while Martha sat in front of the television and watched the soap operas that she so loved. Cassandra tried the soaps for a while, but she couldn't remember from one day to the next whether Eric was a good guy or a bad guy, or whether Sarabeth was pregnant with Josh's or Lorenzo's baby—no, it couldn't be Lorenzo's, he was on the other program. She had long finished the books and magazines that she had brought with her, and she had bought every magazine that she could find in Pecos and had read those too.

It can't be, Cassandra said to herself every afternoon. *I can't be bored. There's so much to do.* And there was, unless you were a houseguest with only minimal responsibilities. But she was becoming restless earlier and earlier in the day, and was beginning to invent excuses to get in the Firebird and make the long drive into Pecos. *I just can't feel this way,* she thought night after night as she lay awake and stared at the ceiling, her mind on the man who slept downstairs. *I love him. He loves me. We're going to be married and live here for the rest of our lives. I like it here. I have to.*

But now it was the middle of November and Cassandra had to admit to herself that she was bored. Now she was restless by noon, and even the nightly poker games she had started could not quell her boredom. Jarratt and his men worked long hours, and she was left alone in the house every day with no one but Martha for company. Did she miss Las Vegas? Not really, Cassandra assured herself. Las Vegas had lost its appeal long before Jarratt had entered her life, and she honestly did not want to go back there. But this was not the meaningful, secure haven that she had thought it would be!

Maybe Jarratt is right, Cassandra admitted to herself one night as she sat alone in the porch swing. It was cold and her breath came in little white puffs, but she was plenty warm in a thick sweater and her lined boots, and she had wanted to come out and stare at the stars and think. *What if I can't fit into Jarratt's life here? I may be just like his mother,* Cassandra acknowledged to herself. *Or maybe no woman, other than one born to it, like Martha, could make it out here. Oh, no, I have to be right,* she wailed to herself. *I have to be able to fit into Jarratt's life out here. If I can't, I'll lose him.*

The creaking of the front door drew Cassandra out of her reverie. Jarratt, also dressed warmly, pulled the door shut behind him and sat down beside her. The swing was wide and their bodies were not touching, but every nerve in Cassandra's body was singing from Jarratt's nearness, and her senses clamored for the touch of his body on hers. When she was this close to him, all of Cassandra's doubts faded. She loved this man, and she would do whatever it took to spend her life with him.

"Thanksgiving is coming up next week," Jarratt commented idly.

"So it is," Cassandra replied casually, wondering if Jarratt was hinting for her to go.

"We don't do much for Thanksgiving," Jarratt said, swinging the porch swing with his foot. "Martha usually roasts a turkey, and we watch the UT–Texas A and M football game with the hands," he volunteered. "I don't think it will compare with the celebrations you usually have in Las Vegas."

"I'm sure it will be fine," Cassandra said quickly, relieved that he did not want her to go before Thanksgiving. "I usually worked on Thanksgiving, to tell you the truth."

"Now, Christmas is another story," Jarratt mused. "Unless a catastrophe strikes, we have all the neighboring

127

ranchers over on Christmas Eve for dinner. Martha does a bang-up job of that every year. Then, on Christmas Day, Mamacita and her new family come up. I guess you usually have to work Christmas too, right?" he added.

"Usually," Cassandra said hollowly, thinking of the lonely Christmas that she could expect to have this year. Obviously Jarratt did not intend for her to stay for the Christmas holidays. Hurt beyond belief, Cassandra would have gotten up and left except that she did not want Jarratt to know how badly her heart was breaking. So although he was becoming friendlier to her, he really did not want her to stay. *Or maybe he really doesn't expect me to,* she thought sadly.

Jarratt hooked his arm around Cassandra and pulled her close, causing tremors of desire to shoot through her. "I miss having you in my bed," he murmured as he nibbled her lips with his own.

"Well, you could always come up and shock Martha," Cassandra whispered against his lips, forgetting her depression for a moment. He forced her head back and claimed her lips hungrily, passionately, demanding that she give of herself as he was going to. Greedily joyfully, Cassandra returned his passionate salute, reaching up with cold fingers and running them through his hair, even though the pain inside her was threatening to rip her apart. How could she ever leave him? she thought desperately, winding her fingers more tightly in his hair.

Jarratt reached up and removed her hands. "Your fingers are cold," he said against her lips.

"Aren't you glad we're not Eskimos?" Cassandra whispered as Jarratt bent his head and reclaimed her lips. They leaned forward and kissed each other hungrily, not touching anywhere else but letting their tangling mouths tell the story. Jarratt's nose was cold and his beard was bristly, and Cassandra knew that her own face was bound to be at least as cold as his, but neither of them cared in the least. This was the first time they had even touched since the afternoon on Lake Mead, and they were so eager for the contact, however fleeting, that the cold air and chilly faces were forgotten.

Finally, when Cassandra thought she wouldn't be able to stand another moment of this exquisite torture, Jarratt pulled away from her mouth and slid his arm around her, holding her close. "No, I don't want to shock Martha," he said heavily, "although I'm tempted!" He held Cassandra and stared up at the winking stars. "Cassandra, are you happy here?" he asked quietly.

"Yes, Jarratt, I'm very happy," she replied quickly, almost flinching at the lie. It hurt her to lie to him, but what could she say?

"Are you sure?" Jarratt asked.

"Yes," Cassandra said, hoping that conviction and not doubt rang in her voice.

Jarratt said nothing, just pulled her face close and kissed her firmly. "Good night, Cassandra," he said gruffly, standing up and going back into the house.

Why wasn't I honest with Jarratt? Cassandra asked herself much later that night as she lay on her back and stared at the ceiling. But she had not been completely dishonest, she thought. When she was with Jarratt all the doubts and fears vanished, and Cassandra was sure that she wanted nothing more than to spend the rest of her life with him on the ranch. *But you're not always so sure,* Cassandra reminded herself as she watched through the window as a cloud covered the moon. *When Jarratt's not around, you would give your eye teeth for something to do. The ranch does bore you, Cassandra, and all the wishing in the world isn't going to change that. Jarratt may have been right, you know. This may not be the life for you.*

CHAPTER EIGHT

Cassandra smoothed the tablecloth over the dining room table and carefully positioned the plates around the table. Martha's turkey, roasting in the oven, filled the house with an enticing aroma, and the sound of the televised Thanksgiving Day parades floated in from the living room. Jarratt and Dusty were out in the barn with a sick calf, but B.C. and Pete were already parked in front of the television, where, with the exception of a brief foray to the dinner table, Cassandra could see that they would probably spend the entire day.

Cassandra had been up at daybreak, restless from another night of broken sleep, but Martha had already been in the kitchen when Cassandra came down, busily basting the huge bird with butter and crumbling cornbread for dressing. Cassandra had made French toast for everyone's breakfast and had helped Martha clean up the kitchen, then Martha had set her to work in the dining room, getting the table ready for the midday dinner. *I guess she's afraid I'll burn down the kitchen this morning,* Cassandra thought as she rubbed her tired eyes with the back of her hand. *And maybe she's right. If I get any sleepier, I'll go to sleep in the middle of dinner.*

If only she could sleep at night! She was tired enough to sleep for a week, but the minute her head hit the pillow and she shut her eyes, images of Jarratt's naked body holding hers as it had in Las Vegas would dance across her eyelids, and a sensual longing so intense that it shook her to the very core of her being would wash over her, leaving her trembling with unrequited longing. It had been four days since Jarratt had kissed her, and the touch of his body, fleeting though it had been, had aroused Cassandra's desire to the point where she would lie awake for hours trying to quell the frustration that now ate at her body as well as her soul. In one kiss Jarratt had reminded her of the perfect accord they had shared in Las Vegas, and Cassandra would have given her soul to experience that passionate delight again.

How much longer can I stand all this? Cassandra asked herself as she wiped the glasses used for company that Martha had asked her to put on the table. Jarratt was as unencouraging as ever, not really talking to her since the night on the porch when he had kissed her so passionately. It was as though he regretted that momentary lapse and all the other ones that went before it. The ranch was as stifling as it had ever been, with the boredom becoming more hideous every day. And now sexual frustration was robbing her of her sleep and making her irritable and snappish during the day. *I ought to go on back to Las Vegas,* she thought involuntarily before she could stop herself, then determinedly pushed that thought from her mind. No, she wouldn't give up yet.

Jarratt and Dusty wandered in and washed up, then parked themselves in front of the television along with B.C. and Pete. *How exciting,* Cassandra thought wryly as the huge inflated cartoon characters of Macy's parade floated across the screen. *But this is what you wanted,* she reminded herself. *This is Jarratt's life, and you wanted to live it with him, and that means putting up with the boring as well as enjoying the rest!*

Martha shuffled in from the kitchen with a huge bowl

of vegetables. Guiltily Cassandra followed her back to the kitchen and helped her bring the rest of the meal in, and dutifully the men trooped to the table. Conversation was limited, and although the food was delicious, the meal was no more exciting than any other dinner that Cassandra had shared with these people in the kitchen. Subconsciously Cassandra had been expecting the day to be exciting, special, festive, and the realization that it was a day like any other came as an unpleasant shock.

After Martha's pecan pie had been dutifully demolished, the men excused themselves and returned to the television, where they eagerly tuned in the University of Texas–Texas A&M football game. Cassandra supposed that it was exciting to natives of Texas, where the longstanding rivalry between the two schools made the game something of an event, but she had always been bored silly by televised football and this game was no exception. After she and Martha had cleaned up the kitchen she retired to her room and tried to get interested in the latest thriller, but she simply could not lose herself in the intricate plot. Throwing down the book in disgust, she pulled on a sweater and ran down the stairs, slipped out of the house, and walked slowly to the pen. She leaned over the fence and watched a couple of calves play with the hay in the trough, then she wandered into the barn and sat down on a bale of hay, drawing out a piece and chewing on the end tentatively. It was surprisingly sweet, and Cassandra sucked at it thoughtfully as she contemplated her future. She knew she should go back to Las Vegas, yet she couldn't bring herself to do it.

Cassandra jumped and whirled as a shadow loomed behind her, then breathed a sigh of relief when Jarratt smiled sardonically and shut the door behind him. "This isn't Las Vegas, you know," he said wryly. "You don't have to be afraid."

"I—I know that," Cassandra stammered, her heart pounding from longing rather than fear. Jarratt was standing right in front of her, almost close enough to touch, and the slight elusive scent of his aftershave tantalized her nostrils. The atmosphere between them was tight with unspoken tension, and frustrated longing spiraled through Cassandra's body in an almost unrepressed wave. She clenched her fists in order to keep from reaching out and caressing Jarratt's firm legs. Fighting down the hopeless longing, she nodded at Jarratt and tried to smile brightly. "Yes, it's much safer out here," she acknowledged quietly.

Jarratt grimaced but said nothing. He sat down beside her on the hay bale and plucked out a straw. Cassandra's nerves had almost reached the screaming point. Without even meaning to, she reached out and ran her hand down Jarratt's arm, feeling the thick crisp hairs as they sprang back from her touch. "Don't do that," Jarratt murmured.

"I have to," Cassandra breathed softly.

Jarratt groaned and reached out with his other hand and drew her close to him, locking onto her mouth with an almost hungry desperation, clearly as helpless in his desire as she was in hers. Eagerly Cassandra returned his feverish embrace, running her hands around his waist and locking her fingers together in the back, holding Jarratt to her with abandoned ardor. The sexual tension that had built between them since Cassandra's arrival on the ranch exploded in this hungry exploration, driving them together with flaming strength. Cassandra moaned as Jarratt found her tender nape and touched it lovingly with his lips and his tongue, and Cassandra let her gentle mouth wander over his eyes and his cheeks with tormenting erotic tenderness. "That feels good, Cassandra," he whispered softly.

"Touch me, Jarratt," Cassandra cried involuntarily, hungry for the thrill of his hands on her body.

With teasing fingers Jarratt explored her breasts and her waist through the thin blouse and lacy bra that she wore, then drew her up with him and ran his hands down the swelling curve of her hips. Cassandra let her hands wander lower, past Jarratt's waist and down his lean side, letting them come to rest on the bones of his hips. They clung together for long minutes, swaying together as they savored the feel of the closeness that they shared.

Slowly Cassandra reached up and unbuttoned the top button of Jarratt's shirt. He ran his hands around her shoulders and reached out and unbuttoned the top buttons of Cassandra's blouse, then reached out and kissed the creamy skin that was exposed. Trembling with anticipation, eager for Jarratt's possession, Cassandra quickly unbuttoned the rest of the buttons on Jarratt's shirt and pushed it off his shoulders, then sighed as Jarratt unhooked the front closure of her bra and captured one of her breasts in his hand, caressing the nipple until it was a tight button. "Oh, Jarratt, I love you," Cassandra murmured.

Jarratt stiffened in her arms and pulled back slightly, his eyes registering his internal as well as his external withdrawal. "My God, what am I thinking of?" he muttered as he gently removed her hands from his chest. He turned to retrieve his shirt from the floor and pulled it back on, buttoning it with shaking fingers. "Making out in the barn in broad daylight like some damned teenager!" His face started to crumple, but by a magnificent act of will he composed himself. "Button your shirt, Cassandra," he said softly. "You'll catch cold."

Cassandra stood silent, fighting back tears. She watched Jarratt button his shirt and stalk out of the barn, banging the door behind him, then put on her bra and blouse. Why did he stop? she asked herself. *Doesn't he love me anymore?* Deeply hurt by Jarratt's defection, she sniffed and dug around in her pocket for a Kleenex. Finding one, she blew her nose loudly and stuffed it back into her pocket. "Damn you, Jarratt Vandenburg," she muttered as she walked back to the house. "I hope I was better than the half-time show on television!"

I'm so bored I think I'll start screaming, Cassandra said to herself as she leaned against the fence and stared into the empty corral. It had been two weeks since Thanksgiving, and Jarratt had been gone since the day after the holiday. The morning after Thanksgiving, after the episode in the barn, Cassandra had been awakened by the sound of movement in the room where Martha and Pete usually slept. Since it was well past eight, Cassandra had gone to investigate and had found Jarratt packing a large suitcase. He had explained that he was going on another buying trip, this time to a ranch in Arizona, and that he didn't know when he would be back. He had not mentioned taking Cassandra and she had not asked, but it had hurt horribly at the time and more even later, when Dusty and Pete had made jokes at the dinner table about all the fun Jarratt was going to have on the Circle T and all the pretty women who came to the parties given by the ranch. He couldn't have made it much plainer, Cassandra had thought. He simply didn't want her in his life. She had bitten her lip to keep from begging to go and had seen him off with a very cool good-bye, and ever since then the boredom and the pain and the restless frustration, further fueled by the scene in the barn, had pushed Cassandra to the snapping point. The ranch was simply a bore. She had read everything there was on the ranch to read, seen enough television to last a lifetime, and played poker until she was sick of it. There was just not enough to do here! How could they all stand it? She had had enough of this place!

Sighing, Cassandra kicked a rock across the yard and into the barn. B.C. was sitting on a pile of hay playing the harmonica. "Whatcha doin', Cass?" he asked as he blew a mournful tune into the harmonica.

"Nothing. Absolutely nothing," Cassandra replied tiredly.

"Me either. Isn't it great to goof off?" B.C. asked as he took a breath. Finding the right note, he continued his mournful ballad.

"You're not busy?" Cassandra asked incredulously. It seemed to her that the men never stopped working.

"Nope, for once I'm not," B.C. admitted. "With Jarratt gone and Dusty in El Paso with his girl friend, it's just me, and after I've done a few chores I'm through."

"Dusty has a girl friend?" Cassandra asked in amazement.

"Yep, he's going with a widow with a teenager girl. Once the girl's out of high school and the woman is free to move, Dusty'll probably marry her."

"I can't imagine," Cassandra replied honestly, giggling a little.

"You'd think it was even funnier if you could see the woman," B.C. replied with amusement. "He's so homely, and she's an absolute knockout."

"Oh, well, it takes all kinds," Cassandra replied sagely, thinking of the unlikeliness of her own love affair with Jarratt. She kicked the rock with her foot. "Damn. I wish I had something to do." She looked over at the saddles on the wall, and the germ of an idea sprang forth in her head. "B.C., are you free for the rest of the day? Would you like to go on a picnic with me?"

"You want to go on a picnic?" B.C. asked doubtfully. "Isn't it a little cold for that?"

"Not if we took the horses," Cassandra enthused. "And we could bundle up. Oh, come on, B.C. It will be fun!"

B.C. nodded reluctantly. "Okay," he replied slowly, "if you want to. You fix the picnic and I'll saddle the horses."

Martha was clearly doubtful about the wisdom of going on a picnic in the middle of December, but Cassandra persuaded her that they would be fine. She fixed a huge picnic lunch, more than they could possibly eat, and packed it into two oversize saddlebags that B.C. had given her. She filled two thermoses with hot coffee and added them to the feast, then bundled up warmly and promised Martha that they wouldn't be late. Jarratt was not due back until tomorrow, so he wouldn't miss her, but Cassandra knew Martha well enough by now to know that the old woman would worry if they were gone for a long time.

B.C. had the horses saddled by the time Cassandra returned to the barn. "We'll go north," he said. "There's a beautiful little valley between two small ranges. You'll like it."

"I'm sure I will," Cassandra replied warmly, thinking that any place was better than the ranch house. They rode north, the cold wind blowing in their faces. B.C. was fun, and they never lacked for something to talk and laugh about for the hour that they rode. Cassandra was glad that B.C. knew where he was going, because the landscape all looked the same to her, and she knew that she would never get back to the house alone.

Cassandra and Dusty rode over a low range, too tall to be called hills but hardly mountains either. As they reached the crest of the hills and were able to see over them, Cassandra gasped at the sheer beauty of the panorama that spread before her. A bubbling stream meandered through the center of the valley, and the usual scrubby growth was supplemented by green grass and some small trees. "Where does the water come from?" she asked.

"Groundwater," B.C. explained, reining his horse in so they could enjoy the view. "It doesn't flow all year around.

137

In fact, this is the first time that I can remember it running this late."

"Let's get closer," Cassandra demanded.

B.C. shook his head. "We'll come back for lunch," he stated. "In the meantime let's ride a little."

Cassandra started to argue but thought better of it. She would get to see the little valley at lunch. She followed B.C. as he dug his heels into the horse's sides and cantered away.

Later Cassandra was not quite sure how it had happened. Surely she should have been able to see B.C. across the sparsely vegetated landscape, and she had become an adequate enough rider in the last six weeks. But B.C. got farther and farther ahead of her, cantering his horse briskly across the hard ground. She would spot him intermittently, and, never dreaming that they could in fact become separated, did not bother to catch up with him. Then Cassandra became absorbed in following the trail of a small jackrabbit across the plains, and when she finally looked ahead, B.C. was gone.

It's all right, Cassandra thought as she rode on at her own pace. *I'll catch him.* But she rode and she rode and she never found B.C. When her stomach started to growl ominously, she checked her watch and discovered that it was after one. *Maybe I better call him,* she thought. *All I need is to get lost.* She cupped her hands and called B.C.'s name loudly. When she got no response, she tried again. Still no B.C. Trying not to panic, she called and called but B.C. did not call back or ride in her direction. When she finally decided that B.C. was too far away to hear her, she kicked the mare in the flank and galloped off in B.C.'s direction. The little horse ran swiftly, but B.C. was nowhere to be found.

After an hour Cassandra gave up. She was lost, hopelessly lost, out in the middle of thousands of acres of desolate ranch country. So what do I do? she asked herself. Surely by now B.C. had realized that she was lost, and would be looking for her. But it might take him several hours to find her, so her best bet would probably be to stay put and wait for him to come.

But there was one other solution. She and B.C. had planned to eat lunch in the little valley, and if she could find her way there, B.C. might have an easier time finding her. Hungry beyond belief, she tied the little mare to a scrubby mesquite bush, then unloaded one of the saddlebags and wolfed down two sandwiches. Her feast barely made a dent in the food in the saddlebags, so B.C. would still be able to eat when he caught up with her.

Cassandra carefully guided the little mare back in the direction from which they had come. She rode steadily for three hours, fighting off panic with her no-nonsense approach to peril, and reasoning that she couldn't be all that far from the valley. She drank part of the coffee in one of the thermoses as she sat in the saddle for a minute and surveyed the surrounding landscape. It looked depressingly unfamiliar, but still Cassandra could not be sure that she had ever seen this particular spot before. Swearing softly, she vowed to ride for another thirty minutes, and if at that point she had not found the little valley, she would stop wherever she was and wait for someone to find her.

Exactly twenty-five minutes later, as Cassandra was about to give up, she spotted a familiar range that jutted up from the ground. Thank God! She had found the valley! Now she knew that she was only a mile or two from the ranch, and that it would be only a little while before B.C. found her. Shivering a little from the cold, Cassandra kicked in her heels and reined the mare toward the range. She had to ride another thirty minutes to reach the range, and then she had to dismount so that the little horse could climb up the steep slopes. *I swear I don't remember it being this steep,* she told herself as she and the small horse stumbled up the side of the hill. *But I wasn't tired this morning.*

Finally! Cassandra thought as she reached the top of the range. She peered over the edge of the hill at the view and stared incredulously, horror growing in her mind. There was no valley. At least not a little valley. There was another range a couple of miles in the opposite direction, but the stream here was muddy and straight, and B.C. was nowhere to be seen. *Oh, my God, where am I?* Cassandra wondered as she looked back over her shoulder. The sun, dipping low in the sky, burned bright orange and warmed Cassandra's face slightly with its feeble rays, but as it slowly sank in the sky, the frightful truth dawned on Cassandra. Unless a miracle happened in the next thirty minutes, she would have to spend the night here alone, with only Jewel for company.

The mare snorted, reminding Cassandra that it had been all day since she had had a drink. Cautiously Cassandra led the little horse down the rocky incline and to the muddy stream. Up close, the water was not sparkling, but was certainly drinkable. Thank goodness, Cassandra thought as she unscrewed the thermos cap and dipped herself a cup. It was wet, and that was all that mattered. She let the horse drink her fill and then tied the reins to a bush, leaving them loose enough to allow for grazing, then removed the saddle and put it on the ground. She guessed that the saddle would be her pillow tonight. Shivering a little, she unpacked another couple of sandwiches and ate them, chasing them down with a cup of hot coffee. By now the sun had set and the temperature was dropping noticeably, and Cassandra realized that her biggest problem tonight would not be food, but warmth.

Quickly, before it became too dark, Cassandra gathered

a pile of dead brush and twigs, putting the kindling on the bottom as she had learned to do in her parents' fireplace. She wished in vain for some larger pieces of wood, but, realizing that those would be few and far between, gathered another pile of brush to use during the night. She searched through the saddlebags and finally found one small book of matches that was half used. Turning her back to the wind, she still burned up three matches before she finally got one to stay lit long enough to set the pile of brush on fire. The kindling did not light as well as she had hoped, but after a few minutes a warm fire was burning brightly. But she realized that her pile of brush was going fast, and that she had gathered nowhere near enough to last the night. It was already quite dark, and since she knew better than to wander away from the light of the fire to gather more brush, she picked up every scrap that she could find. Then, exhausted from the day's exertions, she sat down wearily and stared into the flames. Shivering as a blast of wind caught her, she knew that she was not dressed anywhere near as warm as she needed to be, and that she had a good chance of suffering from severe exposure if her supply of wood gave out before morning. She sat down and stared into the flames, rubbing her hands together and stomping her feet on the hard ground and cursing the impulse that had led her on this ill-fated venture. She lost track of time, marking only the intervals when she had to add her fast-dwindling wood to the fire.

At first Cassandra thought that the hoofbeats that she heard were just in her imagination. She was just hoping that B.C. would find her, that was all. But as the sounds became louder and louder, she raised her head and was astonished to see a horse riding toward her, the rider holding a huge battery lantern high in his hand. The rider rode straight toward her from the direction of the stream, opposite from which she had come. Cassandra jumped up and waved her arms frantically in the light of the fire, although from the speed and determination with which the rider was coming toward her she knew that he must have spotted the fire a long time ago. Thank God, B.C. had found her! she thought as she shook from her shivering. They could ride back to the ranch and she could sleep in the iron bed, her hours out here just a frightening memory. "B.C.!" she called as the rider came within earshot.

"How the hell did you get all the way over here?" Jarratt thundered as he galloped up and climbed off Samson. He pulled out a small portable CB and spoke into it. "I found her," he said, pausing as B.C.'s voice came over the machine, a metallic crackle that Cassandra could not understand. "Yes, she's fine. Just cold," Jarratt added. "No, we can't get back tonight. Too far." Jarratt snapped off the CB and turned to her, his hands on his hips, and Cassandra swallowed convulsively. She had seen Jarratt happy, sad, passionate, and indifferent, but she had never seen him really angry. His dark eyes burned into her and it was all she could do to keep from backing away.

"Wh-what are you doing here?" Cassandra stammered, holding her arms across her chest. "You're supposed to be buying bulls."

"Bulls, hell. Martha called me when B.C. turned up without you. I spent all afternoon flying back to find you, you damn little fool."

"You don't have to swear at me," Cassandra replied with what little tattered dignity she could muster, her shivering becoming worse. "B.C. and I were on a picnic. We got separated and I got lost."

Jarratt advanced on her with his hands poised to grasp her. Frightened, Cassandra stumbled backward and almost fell into the fire, kicking one branch and sending a glitter of sparks up into the air. Jarratt reached out and grabbed her, pulling her away from the fire and into his arms. He held her close, stroking her hair for long minutes as Cassandra drank in the delicious warmth of his body. All too soon he thrust her away and dug around in his oversize saddlebags, producing a huge poncho and settling it over the top of Cassandra's head. "Now, see if you can stay in one place long enough for me to gather up some more wood," he commanded as he picked up a flashlight and walked away.

"You don't have to be nasty," Cassandra replied to his retreating form. Slowly feeling the warmth of the poncho sink in, Cassandra sat down and waited for Jarratt to return. What a man of contradictions! He had been furious with her for getting lost, but he had held her tight and warmed her body until the shivers racking her frame had stopped.

Jarratt returned with a large armful of wood. He dropped it beside the other and went into the woods again, not speaking to Cassandra. He brought in three more armfuls and placed them with the others, then plopped down beside her. "I gather you realize that we'll have to go back in the morning," he said heavily.

"At first I wondered, but the third load of wood convinced me," Cassandra replied sardonically. "Why can't we go back tonight?"

"Because you managed to get over twenty miles from the house," Jarratt said dryly. "Frankly, lady, it was a miracle that I ever found you." He glowered at her. "I guess you know you could have frozen to death," he commented sarcastically.

"The thought had crossed my mind," Cassandra snapped back. "Look, is it really too far to ride back tonight? I'm cold."

"You'd be a helluva lot colder up on the back of that horse," Jarratt shot back. "Look, I've been riding for three hours as fast as Samson could carry me, and I have no desire to get back on him and ride for three more. So unless you want to get back up on Jewel and try to find your way back to the ranch by yourself, I suggest that you shut up and let me rest a little."

"Sor-ry," Cassandra drawled. "You sure know how to treat a lady who has been lost and scared and cold for most of the day."

"You forgot hungry," Jarratt jibed.

"Oh, I'm not hungry," Cassandra said nonchalantly. "I had the food."

"Food? Why didn't you say so?" Jarratt demanded. "I'm starving!"

"You didn't ask," Cassandra replied as she reached over and handed Jarratt the saddlebags. He dove into one and pulled out three sandwiches, wolfed them down in about two bites apiece, and reached for another. "You'd think you hadn't eaten all day," Cassandra said disdainfully as she removed a piece of cake and nibbled it delicately. The cold wind ruffled her hair, but under the poncho she was warm.

"I haven't," Jarratt replied as he ate the fourth sandwich. "At least not since breakfast."

"What happened to your lunch and dinner?" Cassandra asked as she licked her fingers clean.

"We were out until almost three looking at the cattle, and then Martha's call came just as we were ready to sit down to dinner. I drove straight back and saddled Samson. When would I have eaten?" he asked as he rummaged around in the saddlebags for something else to eat.

"There's more cake in the bottom," Cassandra volunteered as she poured herself a cup of coffee from the thermos. The coffee was no longer hot, but Cassandra actually found herself enjoying it.

Or was she enjoying more than just the coffee? she

144

wondered as she sipped the lukewarm brew and stared into the fire. In spite of the harsh words that Jarratt had spoken to her, she had to admit that she was honestly glad to be out here with him, glad to be alone with him away from the ranch and Martha's watchful eye. For some reason the words that she had spoken all those weeks ago in the restaurant in Las Vegas popped into her mind. *Moonlight, a blanket of stars, no one else for miles and miles. Quiet. A man I love.* Well, she had those tonight. And despite the conflict that had grown up between her and Jarratt, she was glad to be with him.

"Cassandra?" Jarratt called softly across the fire.

"Yes, Jarratt?" she asked.

"I'm sorry I was so hard on you when I found you," he said quietly. "It's just that you scared the hell out of me. I could picture you out here cold, and alone, with just that horse for company."

"That's all right," Cassandra replied quietly. "I would have done the same thing to you."

"No, you wouldn't," Jarratt replied. "You would have been patient and kind with me."

"Blame it on your empty stomach," she said lightly, hoping to forestall the tears that she felt welling in her eyes. She had been strong when she had needed to be, and had fended for herself just fine today when she was alone and had to. Then when Jarratt had ridden up and been so angry, she had been angry and defensive in return and had not truly appreciated just what kind of night he had spared her. But now that the anger was over and he was being kind, the fright of the last few hours and the misery that she had almost had to face finally took its toll, and two big tears welled up in Cassandra's eyes and spilled down the front of the poncho. Within seconds she was sobbing uncontrollably, great heaving sobs racking her body as she sat with her head resting on her knees.

"God, Cassandra, I'm sorry," Jarratt exclaimed as he moved to her side and put a gentle hand on the back of her neck. "After all you had been through, and then for me to yell at you! Don't cry, lady, please don't cry." He reached around her and held her to him, cradling her in his arms as he rocked her back and forth. Nevertheless, he let her cry in his arms until her tears were spent.

"I'm sorry," Cassandra hiccoughed as she slowly gained control of her emotions. "I didn't mean to do that."

"I assume that you didn't mean to get lost either," Jarratt replied dryly.

Cassandra shook her head against his shirt front. "We got separated accidentally," she admitted. "I tried to ride back to the little valley that was close to the house. Obviously I didn't make it."

"No, you didn't," Jarratt agreed. "Although by the time you arrived here, you had actually gone full circle and were coming back toward the house. You were just about twenty miles off, that was all."

"Is that why you rode in from that direction?" Cassandra asked as she pulled out of Jarratt's arms, embarrassed. She had made a fool of herself today, first by getting lost and then by crying, and she didn't want to hang all over him any more than she already had, in spite of the warm, sensuous, secure feeling that she had in his arms. Sitting down a few inches away from Jarratt, she picked up a stick and drew little designs in the dirt.

"Yes, I came straight from the house," he acknowledged. We're at the west edge of the ranch. I was going to ride the west third and B.C. the east, and Pete was taking the middle third. We would have looked all night if we'd had to."

"Thank you," Cassandra said sincerely. "I'm sorry I scared you." She looked over at him sitting beside her, and caught him staring at her intently, with a look of smoldering longing in his eyes that he could not extinguish. He reached out for her and slid his arm around her neck, cupping her head with his palm and drawing her to him. He met her lips with his own, drawing the love out of her with tender persuasion. Groaning, Cassandra reached out and pulled him to her, scooting over on the cold hard ground so that they would be even closer. Their mouths entwined, tangling, touching, exploring, until they were breathless. She moaned a little as Jarratt's teeth ground into her lips, but the minor pain was nothing compared to the brilliant delight of being this close to him again.

Without warning Jarratt wrenched away. Tearing his mouth from hers, he put Cassandra a safe distance from him and hunched his legs close to his body, his head resting on his knees. "It's late, Cassandra," he said harshly. "We need to get some rest before the long ride back tomorrow."

"Jarratt, why?" Cassandra whispered as she looked at him in bewilderment. What had made him thrust her from him? Unless he still thought she was trying to seduce him. Although admittedly seduction had been on her mind when she had first come from Las Vegas, tonight that was the furthest thing from her mind. What had just happened between them had been the spontaneous outpouring of her love for him. But if Jarratt did not want her love, she could not force it on him. Quickly wiping the tears from her eyes, she got up and threw a little more brush on the fire, then put the saddlebags away. "Do you have a poncho to sleep in?" she asked Jarratt.

"Better than that," Jarratt replied, standing up and going to his saddle. "I brought a couple of sleeping bags in case I did find you out this far." He pulled out two down sleeping bags that could be packed in a very small space and shook them out to full, although narrow, size. "With the poncho you should be quite warm," he volunteered.

"Thank you," Cassandra said quietly. Separate sleeping bags! Jarratt thought of everything. *He must be really determined not to sleep with me again. Oh, Jarratt, why? Why are you doing this to us?*

Cassandra wandered off for a few moments of privacy and returned to find the sleeping bags spread out on the ground, the pillows to the fire. Jarratt had removed his coat and was in the process of trying to take off a dress shirt. He had unbuttoned it and had pulled it off his shoulders, but the cuff links were small and he was fumbling around with them in the firelight. "Get over here and help me, Cassandra," he demanded harshly. "I'm freezing!"

Cassandra quickly moved to Jarratt's side and began the tedious task of unhooking the cuff links. "What are you doing in a dress shirt?" she asked as she felt around in the semidarkness for the small link. This close she could smell the scent of Jarratt's aftershave and the mingling of his natural musk, and see the shivering of his exposed skin. Without meaning to, she reached out and planted a kiss on his shivering chest.

"Oh, Cassandra, don't do that," Jarratt begged as she removed one cuff link.

"Don't do what?" she replied innocently as she reached out and nibbled his chest lightly. Although deliberate seduction had not been in Cassandra's mind before, she couldn't help but take advantage of Jarratt's touching vulnerability and torment him a little. "You asked me to take these off, didn't you?" Quite slowly she reached for Jarratt's other wrist and drew it to her.

"You know what I mean," Jarratt rasped as she rubbed his fingers against her waist. "God, Cassandra, you're driving me crazy!"

"Good," she replied honestly, unsnapping the other cuff link and drawing the shirt off his broad frame. "You've been driving me crazy for weeks. What on earth were you doing in a dress shirt, anyway?"

"I didn't take time to change," Jarratt admitted as Cassandra wrapped her arms around his naked waist. "I was terrified that something was going to happen to you. Now," he said, pushing her away from him, "we go to bed."

Just at that moment a mournful howl pierced the darkness. "What was that?" Cassandra demanded, leaping back into Jarratt's arms, trembling with terror.

"A coyote," Jarratt replied, cradling Cassandra and rubbing her back lightly. "He's harmless. But I'm not," he groaned, pulling her even closer and holding her against his warm body. She could feel the evidence of his desire against her, and instinctively she moved to further the contact between them.

"I tried, Cassandra," Jarratt whispered as he tilted her head back and covered her mouth with soft, quick kisses. "I tried to stay away from you," he said as he reached around and ran his hands up her back. "I tried to work things out between us before I took you back in my arms," he whispered as he reached forward and started unbuttoning her blouse. "But I simply have to make love to you tonight. I can't help it, Cassandra, I want you too badly to let you sleep alone."

"I'm glad," she whispered softly. "I'm so glad!" She reached out and drew Jarratt's shivering body to her. "I want you so much! But what do we do about the sleeping bags?" she whispered as Jarratt's tongue made a delicious foray into her ear.

"They zip together," Jarratt admitted sheepishly.

"Then let's zip them together before you freeze to death," Cassandra said as she broke away from Jarratt and knelt between the sleeping bags. "What do I do?"

"Hold these ends together," Jarratt commanded as he

quickly unzipped the bags. He started putting the bags together, but the zipper jammed in the cloth and his trembling fingers could not get the fabric worked out.

"Allow me," Cassandra said as she took the tangled segment from Jarratt's shaking hands. As quick as a wink she had freed the zipper and had joined the two sleeping bags together into one. Jarratt jerked off his boots and socks and jumped into the bag, shivering for a moment as Cassandra pulled off her own boots and socks. As the cold air hit her feet she dove into the bag, curling up against Jarratt as she let the warmth of her body warm his cold chest and back.

When he had stopped shivering, Jarratt turned over and kissed her slowly, lazily, nibbling and touching her lips and her face with soft, sensuous love touches. In spite of his earlier passionate outburst, he did not seem in any hurry to culminate their lovemaking, but was content for long moments to touch her face and her neck lovingly. Cassandra understood. In Las Vegas their relationship had been new, fresh, with the flush of first being in love, and their lovemaking had reflected this curious exploration. Tonight was different. They were coming together after being apart for far too long, and they held and touched with the tender poignancy of lovers reunited after a long, painful separation. Tonight they would touch and caress with the sensual familiarity of two lovers who already knew each other's spirit and soul, and who wanted to renew that tender, restoring intimacy. She returned his kisses slowly, warmly, passionately, caressing him with her eyes, her hands, her lips. Cassandra bent her head and touched his chest, now warm again, with her tender tongue.

Jarratt reached out and slid Cassandra's blouse from her shoulders. "You won't need this tonight," he murmured against her lips. "I can keep you warm." He drew

150

the blouse from her body and unhooked her bra, sliding it down her arms and burying his face between her warm breasts. "I've missed the taste of you, and the feel of your warm body against mine in the night," he murmured as he took one nipple into his mouth, tormenting it with his tongue until it was hard to the touch.

Jabs of pleasure shot through Cassandra as he brought his loving kisses to her other breast. "I've missed you too," she murmured as her hands found the small of Jarratt's back and she rubbed small circles into the sinewy muscles there. "I've missed the way you make me feel when you tease me—yes, like that!" she murmured as Jarratt slid down the waistband of her jeans and moved his finger into her navel, caressing it teasingly.

"The better to make love to you, my dear," Jarratt replied as he unzipped her jeans and stripped them down her body.

"Oh, dear, the UT stripper is at it again," Cassandra teased as she pulled the jeans the last few inches down her legs. She burrowed down into the sleeping bag and pulled off her jeans, allowing her fingers to torment Jarratt's stomach and chest ever so lightly on the way back up. "You're going to have to take off your own pants," she told Jarratt as she lowered her hands to his waist. "I don't think I can manage that feat."

Jarratt wiggled down into the sleeping bag and pulled off his jeans, tossing them on top of hers outside the sleeping bag. Quickly, before she could protest, he had rolled on top of her and was gently pushing her back into the soft bag, pinning her gently beneath him. "Got you now," he murmured as he covered her face with warm, moist kisses.

Cassandra jumped a little when the coyote howled again. "Don't worry," Jarratt murmured against her lips. "He's just as frightened of you as you are of him. Enjoy this, Cassandra. We have it all. Moonlight. A blanket of

151

stars. No one else for miles and miles. Quiet. The woman I love."

"You remembered," Cassandra whispered, tears in her eyes.

"Of course I remembered. That's the moment that I fell in love with you," Jarratt whispered softly, covering her face and her neck and her breasts with warm, soft, loving kisses.

Cassandra honestly thought that they had had the ultimate before, but tonight, under the west Texas canopy of stars, they reached heights that she had never dreamed possible, even after Jarratt had come into her life. They touched, they explored with their lips and their fingers, they murmured sweet love-nothings to each other as their excitement grew to an almost unbelievable pitch. Cassandra didn't know if they were actually doing anything differently from before or if the love that was so strong between them was making every caress a tormenting thrill, but as they kissed and touched and probed and caressed, love poured out of every move, drawing her up into an ecstatic spiral that threatened to take her out of herself. Jarratt touched her breasts, her waist, her intimate places, with knowing, gentle fingers, bringing her to the peak of desire that had her begging him with words and caresses to complete their intimacy. Finally he moved over her and they became one, joining together in harmonious, soaring rhythm, responding to a pattern that was a millennium old yet fresh for every pair of lovers. Cassandra tossed beneath him as swirling mists of pleasure threatened to rob her of her very consciousness. Lights flickered behind her eyelids as she closed her eyes and moaned Jarratt's name over and over, crying out softly as the ultimate of passion overtook her and she shook from head to toe from its tremors. Jarratt moaned softly and whispered her name as he joined her on that heady, passionate spiral. Exhausted, tender, spent, he rolled to one side of Cassandra, not breaking the intimate contact of their bodies as he stroked her perspiring body gently.

They made love again in a few minutes, not speaking this time, just holding and touching and loving. This union was not as explosive as the first, but was a gentle, tender salute to the love that grew stronger between them as time passed. Then they lay together and murmured gentle things to each other until Jarratt drifted off to sleep, his head buried deep within the sleeping bag, pillowed between Cassandra's breasts.

Cassandra lay awake for a long time, staring up at the stars. *I know now that he still loves me,* she thought. *He'd have to, to make love to me like that, to hold me with that kind of passion!* She cradled his head between her breasts and stroked his hair gently. *I love you too, Jarratt,* she vowed silently. *And I'm not going to give up. We can make it, you and I, in spite of the ranch and the boredom. I can't help being bored, but I'll do something so that it doesn't tear us apart. We have too much going for us not to make it.* Cassandra's doubts about their future were dispelled. She was doing the right thing by staying and fighting Jarratt for their future. She would never give up now. She would stay at the ranch, forever if need be, until Jarratt was hers.

CHAPTER NINE

Cassandra stretched a little in the saddle and sighed contentedly, gazing at the majestic panorama that spread before her. She and Jarratt had reined in for a few moments to give the horses a breather, and so that they could enjoy the spectacular view of the barren hills, yet another of the small ranges on the Vandenburg ranch, thrusting upward boldly and beautifully. In spite of her day alone on this desolate land, Cassandra had grown to love the barren, windswept landscape more each day, or maybe it was that she so loved the man who lived here. But this morning she did not particularly care which it was. She was in love, and she was delightfully, deliciously sore, and not entirely from riding all of the day before! Her bones ached as much from their intense lovemaking as from the riding, and her face was still slightly bemused from the loving passion that they had shared. Jarratt had awakened her before dawn with a long and tender kiss, and they had made love yet again, buried deep in the warm sleeping bag. Then they had held each other close for a while, and watched together as the sky lightened and the fresh pink sun peeked over the horizon.

Struggling and laughing together, they had pulled on most of their clothes while they were still in the bag, then they had washed their faces in the little stream and eaten the last of the picnic food for breakfast. Jarratt's beard darkened the lower portion of his face and Cassandra was sure that her hair had a million tangles in it, but they were not really too much worse off for their night together in the wild. Almost sadly Cassandra saddled her horse as Jarratt saddled his, and it was with real reluctance that she mounted Jewel to ride away from the valley where she and Jarratt had known such love. Still, they could always go back there to camp, and when their children were older they would bring them to the spot that meant so much to their parents. Cassandra sighed and looked over at Jarratt, love written all over her face. He smiled gently in her direction, then reined Samson to the left and motioned for Cassandra and Jewel to follow. "We better just walk the horses for a few miles," Jarratt cautioned her, kicking Samson into a walk. "They both put in long days yesterday."

"I know," Cassandra replied, giving Jewel's soft neck a gentle pat. "I didn't run her much, but I rode her nearly all day."

"I galloped poor Samson for three hours," Jarratt admitted ruefully. He watched a crow as it circled overhead. "I'm going to have to get on B.C.'s case about taking you out yesterday," Jarratt said firmly. "That was a lamebrain stunt for him to pull."

"Oh, don't get after B.C.," Cassandra said cajolingly. "It wasn't his fault that I got lost."

"It's not just your getting lost," Jarratt replied sternly. "It's the idea of taking you out there in the first place. I wonder what ever possessed him to suggest such a thing?" he added in wonder.

"It wasn't B.C.'s idea," Cassandra said in a small voice.

Jarratt turned to stare at her wonderingly. "Then whose was it?" he asked. "Surely not yours?"

"Yes, it was mine," Cassandra replied sheepishly. "I talked him into it."

"You *what!*" Jarratt yelled, startling Samson into a trot.

"What's the matter with that?" Cassandra asked. "I was bored. I didn't have anything to do, so I—"

"You mean that you actually persuaded B.C. to take you out on a freezing cold day on a picnic because you were bored?" he demanded incredulously, reining in on Samson a little.

"What are you so bent out of shape about?" Cassandra asked indignantly. "Yes, I was bored, so I asked B.C. if he wanted to go on a picnic. He said yes, and we went. Simple as that."

"Simple as that?" Jarratt asked sarcastically. "Simple as that. Only you get lost, and it took hours to find you, not counting the night we had to spend out in the cold, and you worried Martha to death. Furthermore, I was about to wrap up the deal on some of the best cattle I've ever seen and I guess that's shot too! Simple as that, she says. Because she was bored."

"Well, what was I supposed to do?" Cassandra demanded angrily. "Yes, I was bored, I was bored stiff. There wasn't one damned thing to do at the house. Why wouldn't I be bored?" Cassandra caught her breath as Jewel skitted a little and she stared straight ahead in horror. My God, she had just told Jarratt, and told him in the worst way possible how she felt about his home. Oh, Lord, what kind of damage had she just done? She had just admitted to him—no, not admitted, shouted at him, in fact—that she was desperately unhappy at his ranch.

She shifted her eyes to Jarratt and found him staring at her openly, his eyes infinitely sad. "I wondered how long it would take you to come out and admit it to me," he said softly.

"You—you knew?" Cassandra gasped, quieting Jewel when the horse flinched at the sound of Cassandra's voice.

"Of course I knew," Jarratt replied heavily. "I would

156

come in for lunch and see that glazed look in your eye, that anything-but-this look that Mamacita always had in hers. I'd see you riding Jewel in the afternoons when you had already ridden her once that morning. I'd see your car tearing out for Pecos. You tried to hide it, but I knew. And it broke my heart, because I knew then that I could never marry you." Cassandra shook her head and listened in stunned silence as Jarratt continued. "I knew that it was just a matter of time before you became totally disgusted and left for your old life." Jarratt reached up and wiped what looked suspiciously like a tear from his eye. "That day you drove up I was angry because I was trying so hard to forget you, and then there you were. But I thought maybe if you stayed and you saw that you liked it without my trying to convince you to like it, that it just might work. You might be able to stay, and I might be able to marry you. But you have to admit that it hasn't worked, Cassandra."

"No, I won't admit that!" Cassandra cried desperately. "I love you too much to just give up like that!"

"But you didn't just give up like that," Jarratt reminded her sadly. "You followed me to Texas, Cassandra. You tried to live my life here for two solid months. You gave it everything you had, but it just hasn't worked."

"We haven't given it enough of a chance!" Cassandra replied quickly. "How do you know that I won't do better as time goes on?"

Jarratt reined in Samson and got down off the horse, tying him to a bush. Cassandra tied her horse and Jarratt motioned for her to sit beside him on a large, smooth rock. "It's time to be honest with ourselves," Jarratt said seriously as Cassandra warily sat down beside him. "Cassandra, I want the truth," Jarratt said bluntly. "Have you been happy on the ranch?"

"No," Cassandra replied. "At least, not all of the time,"

she amended, hating the sound of her frank confession. "When I'm with you it's wonderful, of course. I forget everything else but my feelings for you and the way I love you."

"And when I'm not around?" Jarratt prompted softly when Cassandra hesitated.

"I'm bored," she admitted, running her fingers through her tangled hair. "There simply is not enough to fill the days. There isn't enough work, or something," she added lamely.

"Like excitement?" Jarratt suggested, rubbing his forehead tiredly.

"No—yes—oh, Jarratt, I don't know!" Cassandra admitted with confusion. "If you're asking if I miss Las Vegas, the answer is no. I honestly don't miss that place at all. But—but I am bored here. I've tried hard not to be. I've helped Martha, I've read, I even watched a couple of those horrible soap operas. I've tried hard not to be bored, and I wish to hell that I weren't. But I am. Tell me, Jarratt, is there anything I can do about it?" She looked at him searchingly, beseechingly, desperately hoping for a solution from him and knowing that it was not forthcoming.

"I wish you weren't bored too, Cassandra," Jarratt said heavily. "I wish it with all my heart. Because no, there isn't anything that you can do about it. I had hoped with all my heart that you would like it out here, that you would come to love the life the way that I do, so that I could ask you to share it with me. I really wanted to do that. But knowing the way you feel about my ranch and my life-style, I can never ask you to share my life here. It wouldn't even be a gamble. It would be a sure loss."

"Jarratt, please, no!" Cassandra begged. "If we could work out something, please!"

"What do you suggest, Cassandra?" Jarratt asked wryly. "Do you want me to give up the ranch?"

"Could you—would you? No, you wouldn't," Cassandra replied woodenly, looking at the set expression on Jarratt's face. "You couldn't. How many generations of Vandenburgs have been here? Four?"

"Five," Jarratt corrected her softly.

"No, you couldn't leave," Cassandra said sadly. "Because if you did, then every time you looked at me you'd think of what you had to give up. You have a responsibility to stay. No, Jarratt. Don't give up the ranch. I'll stay, and I'll learn to cope the best way I know how."

"Damn it, Cassandra, don't you see? You'll never be able to make it! It took Mamacita fourteen years of misery to admit that she couldn't stand the life. Do you think you could stand fourteen years of the last two months?"

"I don't know!" Cassandra cried in anguish. "Oh, Jarratt, we can't do this! What about last night?"

"Last night was the most beautiful night of my life," Jarratt admitted honestly, his face cloaked in a bitter sadness. "That's why this is just that much harder today. But we're not going to make it, Cassandra. Oh, we'd have nights like last night all right, but then we'd have mornings like this one, and sooner or later it would tear us both into little pieces. We can't do that to ourselves."

"I'm not going back to Las Vegas, Jarratt," Cassandra said softly, her voice shaking with heartbreak. "I just can't stand to end it this way."

Jarratt stood up and untied his horse. "I'm not throwing you out, Cassandra," he said bitterly. "Although why you want to drag out the torment is quite frankly beyond me." He untied Jewel and threw the reins in Cassandra's lap. "Come on," he commanded. "We have two more hours of riding ahead of us."

In the week and a half that followed, Cassandra often wondered why she didn't just leave as Jarratt wanted her to. She certainly had nothing to gain by staying. Jarratt had made that painfully clear during their discussion on the way back from their night out. They had ridden back to the house in silence, a sad, disappointed anger enveloping them both in a bitter dark cloud. They had not spoken to each other since the argument, and Jarratt was short-tempered and rude to everyone else on the ranch, even raising his voice to Martha. Cassandra was quiet and withdrawn, not bothering to hide the circles under her eyes with makeup, and frequently not even bothering to organize her beloved poker game after supper. She cried herself to sleep night after night, sobbing quietly into her pillow lest Martha and Pete hear her and come to see if she was all right. At first Martha and the men were amused by the lovers' quarrel, but when the days passed and it became obvious that the disagreement, whatever the subject, had been serious, they became concerned and increasingly uneasy about the rift between Cassandra and Jarratt and uncomfortable in the presence of the feuding lovers. Meals became ordeals of strained silence, with B.C. and Dusty forced to carry the conversation while Cassandra and Jarratt glowered at each other bitterly and Martha and Pete looked on with bewilderment. What on earth had happened to make Jarratt and his houseguest so bitterly furious with each other?

Cassandra took long walks in the afternoons, often kicking a rock absently with her foot as she thought about her and Jarratt. She had to be honest with him; she had had no choice. To have been otherwise would have been horribly wrong. Yes, she was bored. She didn't like the quiet life on the ranch. But even as she had romantic daydreams of Jarratt selling the ranch and moving with her to the city, she knew that it would never happen. It was not that he loved the ranch more than he loved her. He loved her deeply. But the ranch was his legacy as a

Vandenburg, and it had been his whole life for thirty-one years. If he had to give it up, they would always have that between them. Try though she did, Cassandra simply could not come up with any sort of solution to their heartbreaking dilemma. She had to go, and he had to stay. She knew that she should pack her bags and leave, that it was tearing them both apart for her to stay here at the ranch, but she simply could not bring herself to take out the suitcases and put her clothes into them. Nearing the ranch house, she stared at the long dusty road that disappeared over the horizon. She knew that when she drove off the ranch for the last time, she would never see Jarratt again. And she could not stand the thought of that.

Cassandra opened the front door and banged it shut behind her, startling Martha, who was on a footstool digging high up in a front closet. The little old lady jumped, lost her footing, and slipped from the precarious footstool. Moving swiftly, Cassandra ran forward and held out her arms, breaking Martha's fall although Martha caused Cassandra to lose her balance and they both fell to the floor. The old lady got up and extended her hand to Cassandra, pulling her up from the hard floor. "Thanks," Martha said gruffly. "That could have hurt."

"I'm sorry I scared you," Cassandra apologized, stretching a little and brushing off her clothes. "What were you doing up on that stool?"

"Digging out the Christmas decorations," Martha replied. "Jarratt's big party is in three days. I can't say why he's botherin' this year, though, the way he's been actin' lately."

Cassandra shrugged lamely. "I guess I haven't helped," she said quietly. "Now, if you'll show me what you want out of the closet I'll get it out for you," she volunteered as she climbed up on the footstool.

Martha looked ready to argue, but Cassandra was already pawing around in the closet. "We need the boxes in the back," she told Cassandra. "The ones with the ornaments and lights in them."

Obediently Cassandra handed down the boxes, then Martha, realizing that she was on to a good thing, took Cassandra around the house gathering up all of the Christmas paraphernalia. Cassandra worked gladly, eager to help Martha and to get her mind off the heartbreak of her doomed relationship with Jarratt. Martha had stored decorations in every corner of the house, even in the attic, and by the end of the day she and Cassandra had appropriated the dining room table as a work station and had stacked an unbelievable pile of lights, tinsel, and baubles there. Cassandra cooed over an earthenware manger scene that Jarratt's mother must have left for Jarratt, and she laughed sadly at some of the handmade ornaments that Jarratt himself must have made as a child.

"Martha, did you say that the party was in three days?" Cassandra asked that evening as they were loading the dishwasher. Dinner had been the usual strained torture, with Jarratt even more unreachable than ever, and Cassandra had been almost glad when he had left the room.

"Yes, it is," Martha replied gruffly. "And I know you're wonderin' how I'm going to get it all done." Cassandra nodded. "I've been wonderin' the same thing myself. Rheumatism's been actin' up some."

"If you wouldn't be offended, how about letting me help?" Cassandra asked slowly. "I used to entertain quite a bit in Las Vegas. Although I promise that I'll let you cut up the chicken," she added impishly, an honest grin on her face for the first time in days.

"All right, I'll cut up the chicken," Martha agreed, the faintest hint of a smile on her face. "But you don't have to help if you don't want to," she added.

"Oh, I want to help," Cassandra said quickly, thinking

162

that if she were working, she would not brood about Jarratt. She looked at Martha almost pleadingly. "Please, let me help," she added. This would be her first and last Christmas with Jarratt, her only chance to share with the man she loved the season of ultimate love, and she desperately wanted to spend it with him.

"Is this what you city folks call therapy?" Martha asked perceptively.

"Oh, Martha, does it show?" Cassandra asked sadly.

Martha nodded grimly. "And I'm real sorry, Miss Howard. Just real sorry." The old woman reached out and patted Cassandra on the arm, then left the room quickly, as though embarrassed by her excessive display of emotion.

Cassandra plunged into Christmas preparations with fervor, even though her heart was breaking. Martha pretty well gave her carte blanche, merely pointing out to her a few of the traditions, such as the manger scene on the mantel, that absolutely had to be adhered to. Otherwise Cassandra was pretty much able to decorate the house any way she pleased. Discovering a flair she didn't realize that she possessed, she tied together sheafs of mistletoe, baubles, and brightly colored ribbons and hung them on all the doors, even framing the manger scene on the mantel with greenery that she had collected from the outdoors. She learned that the tiny scene had been Jarratt's grandmother's, and so paid special care to adjust the pieces just right, thinking that if circumstances had been different that the manger scene would have gone to one of her own children.

The next day Cassandra borrowed Pete's truck and drove into Pecos, bringing back the biggest tree on sale in the tiny town and supervising Dusty and B.C. as they placed it in the stand. She hauled out the party dishes and ran them through the dishwasher, stopping the machine in midcycle so that she could wipe the clear crystal plates until they sparkled, hoping that Jarratt would be proud of the table that she and Martha set, knowing that it would be the last time she would ever set one for him. She polished the silver and washed and ironed the party napkins.

With Martha's permission she called Sharon, who was recovering very nicely, and asked her for her excellent punch recipe and several of her best hors d'oeuvres suggestions, remembering with a pang that Jarratt had enjoyed some similar ones at one of the buffets in Las Vegas. She and Martha had a lively debate over which tablecloth to use on the table the night of the party, and Martha finally gave in and agreed to use a white lace tablecloth with a red lining instead of the usual Christmas cloth with mistletoe and holly printed on the ends. Martha suggested that Cassandra use Jarratt's mother's candlabra and light the dining room entirely by candlelight. To Cassandra's eternal amazement, although Martha was to do the actual cooking, she actually consulted Cassandra on the menu and agreed that it would be nicer to prepare a light buffet supper, with a variety of finger foods and light dishes, rather than the usual heavy sit-down dinner that Martha was accustomed to preparing. As they planned the menu Cassandra wondered sadly if they would go back to the traditional dinner next year, or if she would leave that one small mark on the Vandenburg family tradition.

The day of the party Cassandra peeled what seemed like tons of vegetables and put together several large bowls of dip under Martha's watchful eye, and later that afternoon they assembled the delicious hors d'oeuvres. When the work was done Cassandra climbed the stairs wearily and packed her suitcases, her lips trembling as she fought back tears. She didn't know if she would actually leave tomorrow, but she knew she had to leave soon, although the mere thought broke her heart.

* * *

Cassandra peered into the mirror as she generously coated her eyelashes with mascara. The circles under her eyes had been covered with makeup, but the telltale sadness in them was still there. She knew that her love affair with Jarratt was hopeless, and that she would be leaving the following morning. But tonight she would store up a few more memories to take back with her to Las Vegas. Tonight was Jarratt's party, and she would meet some of his friends and see him with them. She would cherish these memories of Jarratt as she would all of the others that she had stored since that fateful night at the Tropical Paradise.

And what would Jarratt's friends think of the little hothouse flower from Las Vegas? A small smile touched Cassandra's lips as she slipped into a glamorous off-the-shoulder party dress, knee-length yet with all the dressy sophistication that she could want. The dress was oyster, and the silk fabric shimmered in the light of her bedroom. The effect would be even more striking in the dining room in the glow of the candlelight. She finished her makeup, not stinting on the color, hoping to hide the pale sadness in her face, then brushed her hair into its usual taffy mane. It had grown even longer in her two and a half months here, and had become a virtual aureole around her face and shoulders. Liberally spraying herself with perfume, she went downstairs, ready to meet Jarratt's friends.

Several couples had already arrived, so Cassandra was spared the torture of being in the room alone with Jarratt. His eyes widened as she walked into the room, and Cassandra realized that he had never seen her this dressed up, even during the time they spent in Las Vegas. His hostility put aside for the evening, he introduced her to the people in the room and mixed her a tequila sunrise. Cassandra sat down and struck up a conversation with one of the young

165

wives, a former schoolteacher who was now a full-time ranch wife. She was very nice, but Cassandra found herself almost bitterly jealous of her. She seemed so content.

As the room filled and the party began in earnest, Cassandra found herself watching these people from the sidelines, certainly participating in the party but not becoming the life of it as she usually did. The men were urbane and educated, only their work muscles and their choices of conversation giving them away as ranchers. The wives were not out-and-out glamorous, but they possessed a certain chic that Cassandra frankly was surprised to find. Their interests were cosmopolitan and well-informed, and their attitudes were not in the least provincial. These people were like Jarratt, every bit as sophisticated as the biggest high roller in Las Vegas. They were ranchers because they loved the life, just as Jarratt did. *I could have fit in with these people,* she thought sadly. *I like them, and I could have made friends here. If only I could have liked the ranch itself. Do the other wives ever get bored? What do they do for fun?*

After drinks had been served the party slowly drifted toward the dining room. Cassandra discreetly slipped out and helped Martha arrange the buffet on the table, then wrapped a towel around her dress and mixed the tangy champagne punch. The women expressed delight at the assortment of delicacies to eat, causing Cassandra to wonder privately how many diets were being cheerfully blown tonight. The men piled their plates full, and she noted with amusement that over half of them slipped back into the dining room for more. Cassandra, while not serving as hostess, still managed to help Martha with the party and yet spend plenty of time as a guest.

Finally one of the younger wives, obviously curious, asked Cassandra where she was from. When she admitted that she was from Las Vegas and that she was a dealer, some of the wives began asking her questions about her life and soon she was the middle of a small circle of women, answering questions about her "glamorous career." A couple of the husbands became interested, and pretty soon everyone at the party was asking her questions about Las Vegas and all the things that she had seen and done there. As she listened to herself, Cassandra realized that her life really had been quite glamorous, and she could see how Jarratt might think that she would want to go back to it sooner or later. *If only he knew,* she thought sadly. But he did know, she reminded herself. He knew the most important fact of all. He might not know how she really felt about Las Vegas, but he knew that she would never last at the ranch.

The party lasted until well past eleven. Finally, realizing that they had long drives to make, the couples straggled out to their cars, and as Jarratt wished them all good night and Merry Christmas from the front porch, Cassandra kicked off her shoes and cleared the dining room table. Martha had already run one set of dishes in the dishwasher, so Cassandra unloaded those and loaded up another dirty batch, stacking the rest in the sink to be dealt with in the morning. She stripped off the lace tablecloth, and stuffed it in the washing machine, leaving the red lining to wash tomorrow. She was in the dining room removing the candles from the holders when she heard the last car drive off and Jarratt walk back through the house. He entered the study and shut the door behind him.

So we're back to the Cold War, Cassandra thought bitterly as she climbed the stairs to her bedroom. *He couldn't even say good night to me. Damn him, anyway.* She sat down on the stool in front of her mirror and started creaming off her makeup. She had just finished and was about to take off her dress when her door creaked open. Cassandra peered around, prepared to tell Martha good night, when Jarratt stuck his head around the door. "Cassandra? May I come in?"

"Sure," she replied, confused. After all these weeks, what was Jarratt doing coming to her room?

He stepped inside and closed the door behind him. "I won't stay long," he said softly, perching on the edge of the bed. This close, Cassandra could smell the elusive scent of his aftershave, and her senses started screaming for him again. Jarratt looked up at her hesitantly. "I just wanted to thank you for helping Martha with the party tonight," he said. "It's the best party this ranch has ever seen."

Cassandra shrugged. "It was easy," she said simply. "I've always done a lot of entertaining." She glanced toward the thin wall that separated her room from Pete and Martha's, wondering if the conversation could be heard through the wall.

"I sent Pete and Martha on home tonight," Jarratt said suddenly, accurately interpreting Cassandra's glance. "I figured they needed to get back to their own place. Besides, we're not fooling anybody anymore."

"I know that," Cassandra said sadly. "Martha already said something to me."

"She's a sharp old lady," Jarratt replied. "And B.C. and Dusty know."

"How did they feel about it?" Cassandra asked quietly, trying not to cry.

"They feel sorry for us. For both of us," Jarratt said quietly.

Cassandra's composure cracked at that expression of Jarratt's friends' concern for them. "Oh, Jarratt, what are we going to do?" she cried as two big tears rolled down her cheeks.

"Oh, Cass, please don't cry, please," Jarratt pleaded as he reached out and took her into his arms. Her bitter tears wet his shirt front and ran down her cheeks. He rocked her comfortingly in his arms, tears of his own running down his cheeks and dripping into her hair. Cassandra and Jarratt cried for long minutes in each other's arms, lovers hopelessly crossed, not by the stars, but by circumstances that neither could overcome.

Finally Cassandra raised her head. "Make love to me, Jarratt," she whispered, her eyes full of tears. "Once more before I go. Above all, I need that tonight."

"So do I," Jarratt murmured as he stood Cassandra between his knees and wiped the tears from his eyes and her own. "But you have to stop crying."

Cassandra nodded, sniffing, a glimmer of a smile fleetingly crossing her face. She reached out and wiped the last tear from Jarratt's cheek. "You're right," she said. "No tears." She moved closer to Jarratt and started the age-old ritual, taking off his tie and unbuttoning his shirt one button at a time. When she had done that she slowly pushed the shirt from his shouders and laid it on the chair beside the bed. Tonight Jarratt was wearing an undershirt, and she reached down and pulled it over his head in one simple motion.

"Been taking lessons, I see," Jarratt smiled approvingly.

Cassandra bent forward and kissed his chest with tender lips. "All kinds of lessons," she acknowledged as she nibbled the sensitive skin of his chest. Then she sought his mouth with her own, bending down with her lips and capturing his mouth with hers, pouring all the love that she could into her tender embrace. She knew that this was the last time that she and Jarratt would ever make love, and she wanted to give him enough love to last him a lifetime. Without breaking the kiss, Jarratt reached up and unzipped Cassandra's dress, but instead of stripping it off her body, he very tenderly removed it, so that it would not be damaged in any way. That done, he eased Cassandra away from him and removed the rest of his clothes. Cassandra drank in the sight of the hard, tanned, male body, knowing that this would be the last time she would ever see Jarratt in this vulnerable state.

Jarratt reached out and tenderly removed the rest of her clothing. "Just let me look at you," he commanded as he drank in the sight of her passionate, lovely body. "I want to see you so I'll never forget."

"Then don't turn out the light," Cassandra murmured as she melted into Jarratt's arms. They held each other gently for a moment, drinking in the sight, storing up a memory that would have to last them the rest of their lives. Then slowly they began to touch each other, gently, tenderly, giving just as much love as they possibly could. First their lips met in a tender caress, then they covered each other's faces with warm, moist, gentle kisses. Jarratt nibbled Cassandra's ears until she was squirming, then carried his intense assault lower, covering her breasts with his warmly sensual lips, bringing both of her nipples to hard peaks of excitement. His hands and his mouth crept lower, bringing a message of love and longing, promising Cassandra all of his passion. When he had brought her to the edge of the precipice, she pushed him back on the bed and proceeded to do the same to him, covering his body with the same kind of loving embrace that he had given her. She nibbled at his ear and kissed his eyelids, then caressed his nipples until he was moaning, and her eyes stung with her unshed tears. Then she shifted her body to cover his and completed their union herself, pouring every ounce of her passion into every movement of her body.

It would have been hard to say who gave the most love that night. Wordlessly, desperately, Jarratt and Cassandra poured their hearts into their lovemaking, each trying to give to that one last expression of love. They exchanged tenderness, passion, devotion—everything that they would have spent a lifetime sharing. Cassandra made love to Jarratt for long moments, giving him her very soul which threatened to dissolve inside her. Then Jarratt rolled her onto her back and made love to her selflessly, giving all of himself, holding nothing in reserve. When they reached the ultimate together, they discovered that that wasn't enough, so they rested in each other's arms and in a few minutes began the ritual again, loving and holding each other and sharing their passion in fevered desperation, as if they could capture these precious moments and hold them fast in time.

Jarrett, exhausted, finally fell into a deep, peaceful sleep. Cassandra, cradled in his arms, stared with haunted eyes out the window into the chilly gray dawn. *I'm leaving today*, she thought. *Now. Before I tear him apart any further.* Although she had not cried as they had made such bittersweet love, tears began to well in her eyes and streamed down her cheeks as she turned to look into the sleeping face of the man she loved so much. She tentatively moved her hand to touch his face, but dropped it onto the sheet. She couldn't bear to feel his skin, so warm and vibrant beneath her fingers. If she did, she would never be able to leave him. "Oh, Jarrett, I have to go. I love you so much, but if I stay we'll destroy each other. We'll end up hating each other for the hurt we'll inflict. Jarratt, I'm sorry. I tried, I really did," she whispered.

Slowly, so as not to awaken him, she slipped out of the bed and found a clean pair of jeans and a shirt. She pulled on her clothes and swiftly removed the suitcases she had packed the day before. As she checked through the bureau drawers, she came across the tiny jewelry box in the bottom drawer. She hesitated, then withdrew the diamond heart and put it on, dropping it under her shirt. She had no reason not to wear it now. She pulled on her boots, and stifling her sobs, she crept out the door, carrying her suitcases down the stairs. She hadn't even kissed him good-bye.

As she shoved open the front door Cassandra heard the door from the kitchen creak open, and Martha stuck her head out. "What are you doin'," she demanded, noting with sadness the misery in Cassandra's face and the tears cascading down her cheeks.

"I have to go, Martha," Cassandra replied, dropping her suitcases to give the old woman, whom she had come to love, a quick hug. "I don't have any choice."

"I'm real sorry, hon," Martha said softly, her wrinkled old face wreathed with concern. "Isn't there anything you can do?"

Cassandra shook her head. "He knows I'm going. Take care of him for me, Martha." She sobbed as she picked up her suitcases and walked out the front door.

CHAPTER TEN

Cassandra slipped one foot out of her high-heeled sandal and rubbed it against her other foot. Thank God, this shift was almost finished and then she would be off for a couple of days. The blaring music in the casino was frankly giving her a headache, and she longed for nothing more than to go home and have a long soak in the tub, then crawl into bed and seek the blessed oblivion of sleep. She collected her bets and dealt another hand, sourly reflecting that she was right back where she had been last fall, dealing blackjack in a damned smoky casino. Oh, well. She would have to be patient. A year or two and she would be out of the casino for good. She had signed up at the local university for a couple of courses that the real estate school had recommended, then when she was finished with those courses she could start the classes for her real estate license. She had found the courses hard going after so many years out of school, but they were a definite challenge, and something to keep her mind off those weeks in Texas, and the man she had left behind there.

Pushing thoughts of Jarratt from her mind, Cassandra dealt the next hand and firmly vowed to think of other things. The casino was not very busy, which was typical of February, and Cassandra longed to take the vacation to New York that she had planned back in the fall. But she had taken off too much time already in going to Texas to try to see if she and Jarratt could have in fact made a go of life together there. Jarratt. Damn it, couldn't she ever stop thinking about him? Would she ever be able to forget the compelling rancher who had so completely enslaved her heart? Sighing, she greeted pit security with relief as they unlocked the drop box and thus relieved her for the shift.

Gratefully she escaped to the break room, grabbed her coat, and fled the hotel, driving home quickly in the cold desert air. There she tiredly sank into a hot bath and collapsed into bed, staring up at the ceiling for a few moments as she always did, remembering the tall rancher that she had left behind. When she had first come back, she had lain awake for long nights thinking of Jarratt, but mercifully exhaustion from all the sleepless nights and from the added load of the courses had taken its toll, and lately Cassandra had fallen quickly into a deep dreamless slumber, going to sleep almost the minute her head hit the pillow.

The next day Cassandra enjoyed a leisurely breakfast and read through the paper, then she tackled her coursework for the better part of the day. Definitely business math was not the easiest subject in the world to master! Oh, well, it sure beat boredom, Cassandra thought as she finally shut the heavy textbook and put away her papers. It was already late in the afternoon, and she would have to fix something to eat soon. She remembered how surprised she had been when she first came back to Las Vegas to find that the boredom that she had been fleeing in Texas had followed her here, at least for the first few days. Then she had resumed her job at the casino and had started the courses at the university, and she had gone back to being her old busy self, except for the constant ache of missing Jarratt with every breath she took.

Yes, it's good to be active, Cassandra thought as she

pulled on her coat and bounced out of the condominium. *I have to have something to do, something to fill the days. Like dealing,* she thought as she walked down the row of condominiums. Sharon's condo had sold to a nice retired couple, and, according to her last letter, she had found a job in a lawyer's office. Cassandra was delighted that Sharon had something to do with herself now. *She needed something to do just like I do,* Cassandra thought. *I have to be dealing, or studying, or going somewhere, or entertaining. I simply was not cut out for the simple life.*

Cassandra wandered down the sidewalk, reliving her months on Jarratt's ranch. Was there anything that she could have done differently? How had she felt about life there? She kicked an empty beer can down the street and picked apart everything that had happened to her there. Did she hate the ranch itself? Or was it just that she had had nothing to do there? Idly she turned and retraced her steps to her condominium, wondering why she was conducting this postmortem yet knowing that she was powerless to stop herself.

Several hours later, after Cassandra had fixed herself a sandwich and was curled up on her sofa with a glass of wine, she again examined those weeks at Jarratt's ranch. Yes, she had been bored, but it wasn't because she didn't like the ranch life itself. She honestly had. She had loved the peaceful evenings playing poker with the men, and she had loved the horses and sitting on the porch swing out under the stars. She had not even minded the smell of the cows that Jarratt continually brought in with him. But she had had nothing really to do. The house was large, but between her and Martha they could have it clean in three hours, and the men didn't mess it up much anyway. She had not done much cooking, since she really didn't know how. She had no hobbies to fill the time or pass the hours. Yet she had to admit to herself that even if she had been

175

busy from sunup to sundown, that she would never have made it there. Domesticity simply was not the answer for her. But she knew that if Jarratt called her to come back to the ranch, she would go instantly, knowing that she would be miserable simply because she missed him so much. She was momentarily tempted to pick up the telephone and call him, but she resisted the impulse. Why make them both more unhappy than they already were?

Cassandra sighed as she finished her glass of wine. She had to admit to herself that even if she had known how sadly her love affair with Jarratt was going to turn out she still would have gone with him that night at the Tropical Paradise. She would not have wanted to miss loving him, even if it was for only a little while. She glanced over at the pile of books on the coffee table and thought about her future. She would get her real estate license, and then she would get out of Las Vegas. Maybe she could move to Phoenix, or Albuquerque, or somewhere in the South, somewhere away from the fast lane, and she could start over. Maybe she could even love someone someday. *No, she thought, that's hoping for too much. I'll never be able to fill the void that Jarratt left. It would be grossly unfair to another man to ask him to love me when I could never return his love. But it was worth it, Jarratt. It was worth it loving you.*

Cassandra studied hard on her two days off, then reported to the casino as she always did. There were the usual selection of tourists, lookers, high rollers, and players to keep her busy, and the hours of her shift sped by. Cassandra, dealing cards with one part of her mind and going over her problems with the other, failed to notice the tall dark-haired cowboy in the expensive western suit who strode into the casino. He looked through the pit anxiously, his gaze caught and riveted by the sight of the taffy-colored head bent over the table, a frown of concentration

176

marring her sexy face. The cowboy gazed at her for long minutes, drinking in the sight of her as a starving man would food, then he headed for the cashier as a huge grin of relief burst forth on his face.

Cassandra stifled a yawn and shuffled the deck. *Just one more hour,* she thought as she dealt. Now what was that the professor had said about business loans not being deductible in certain cases? She dealt the cards around the table, then stopped and stared at the man in third base, nearly dropping her deck as Jarratt laid a two-hundred-dollar bet, smiling and winking at her broadly. *What on earth?* Cassandra wondered as the players picked up their cards. She couldn't believe it. Jarratt was here in Las Vegas, at her table, and he was gambling! He was gambling a lot of money! And he was smiling at her! What was going on?

Her heart beat like a trip-hammer as Cassandra dealt more cards to the people who wanted them. Then they showed their hands. Dealer's hand was eighteen. Pretty good. She collected chips around the table, staring with astonishment when Jarratt showed her his hand. He had twenty. He had actually won! Grinning with delight, Cassandra pushed him his chips and dealt again. Her concentration completely ruined, Cassandra forgot everything she ever knew about gambling. She played her hand, and was honestly delighted that Jarratt had won yet again. As she dealt again she noticed that he had placed a thousand-dollar bet. *Oh, Jarratt, I hope you know what you're doing,* she thought as she dealt him his cards. She dealt more cards to those who wanted them, then turned over her own hand. It was a twenty. Damn! Jarratt was sure to lose this one. She showed her hand and began to collect chips from the others. As she reached Jarratt he held out his cards and grinned wickedly. *My God,* she thought excitedly. Jarratt was holding a blackjack!

Jarratt collected his winnings and left the game, wandering off toward the cashier's cage. Completely dumbfounded, Cassandra watched him leave with an emotion close to hysteria. What was he doing in Las Vegas at her table? What was he doing winning, for heaven's sake? *Jarratt, come back*, she thought. But he would be back. The loving expression on his face had told her that.

Cassandra dealt the cards with shaking fingers, her mind on Jarratt, not noticing when her pit boss approached her. "Cassandra?" he asked at her elbow.

"Yeah, Joe?" she replied, startled.

"That guy who was at your table, the one who just won a lot of money, he wants to know if you'll go out with him after your shift. For a drink, you know. I told him you don't usually go in for that sort of thing, but he was pretty sure you would."

A wide smile broke out on Cassandra's face. "Ask him what he wants to drink, and when."

Joe's mouth fell open, but he obediently trotted back to his station. He came back a few minutes later, even more confused. "He says that he wants to have a cup of coffee with you tomorrow morning, and every morning for the rest of your life."

So Jarratt had decided to take the gamble after all! He was going to give their love a chance! The problems of life on the ranch temporarily forgotten, Cassandra let loose with a joyous whoop and turned around and kissed Joe on both cheeks. As Joe's eyes flew open, she motioned the relief dealer over. "Take this table," she demanded. "Joe, I resign. I'll be back to see you someday, when I bring my kids and show them where Mommy used to work." She ran through the casino, dodging the other tables and the milling crowd, and threw herself into Jarratt's arms, wrapping her arms around his waist and holding him

178

close. "Oh, Jarratt, I love you," she whispered, her eyes shimmering with tears of joy.

"I gather you want that cup of coffee?" he laughed, bending his head and kissing her long and passionately right in the middle of the casino. Cassandra melted into him, tears of joy wetting her eyelids.

They broke apart guiltily as they realized that they were right in the middle of the casino and looked around warily. When they realized that the dedicated gamblers had not even noticed their passionate greeting, they laughed out loud and left the casino, their hands clasped tightly together. Cassandra entered the break room for one last time and emptied her locker, grateful that she had brought a white lace dress to wear tonight to a baby shower planned for one of the dealers. She tossed the baby gift on the table, figuring that the mother-to-be would understand, and slipped into the white dress. She and Jarratt left the hotel, stowed her things in her Firebird and, holding hands, they headed up the Strip.

The cold wind whistled down the Strip, bringing Cassandra off her excited high and reminding her of reality. Jarratt had proposed, and she had accepted, but before them still lay every problem that had faced them in Texas. Nothing had changed. She still had life on Jarratt's ranch to cope with, and they still had a lot of problems to work out before they were assured of happiness.

Cassandra reached out and touched Jarratt's sleeve with her free hand. Immediately he tucked her cold fingers in between his arm and his body, protecting them with his warmth. "I see you have on the diamond heart," Jarratt said softly. "You never wore it in Texas."

"It was a good-bye gift, remember?" Cassandra replied. "I didn't wear it until I was convinced that it really was good-bye."

Jarratt reached up and took off the necklace and put it into his pocket. "Then you can't wear it now, can you?"

Cassandra shook her head happily as they continued walking.

"Jarratt?" Cassandra said quietly.

"Yes, Cassandra?" Jarratt replied, stopping in his tracks and bending to kiss her cold lips.

"What made you come back?" she asked softly.

Jarratt took her hand in his and walked down the Strip, not speaking for a few minutes. The bright, gaudy lights of the Strip hid nothing of his expression from her, and his heady grin of a few minutes ago faded, to be replaced by an expression that was almost grim. "I just couldn't stand it without you," he confessed finally. "Nothing had any meaning anymore. My work was nothing. My ranch was a prison. My friends simply weren't enough. Frankly, Cassandra, it all doesn't mean a damn anymore without you."

"I'm sorry," Cassandra replied quietly. "But I'm glad too," she confessed as Jarratt turned to stare at her in astonishment. "I feel that way about you too, you know."

Jarratt stopped and kissed her again, this time even more passionately. "I could definitely get used to this," he murmured wickedly against her lips. "Every morning for the rest of my life!" He looked around at the brightly lit Strip. "I just hope I can get used to the rest of Las Vegas," he murmured thoughtfully.

"Why should you have to?" Cassandra asked in puzzlement.

"Well, now that I've sold the ranch and am moving here—"

"You sold the ranch!" Cassandra exploded, whirling around and facing Jarratt. "You have to be kidding! You can't do that!"

"I signed the papers yesterday," Jarratt replied calmly. "Got a lot for it too. It's prime grazing land."

180

"Jarratt, how could you?" Cassandra wailed, tears welling in her eyes. "There have been Vandenburgs there for five generations! Your kids were going to be the sixth."

"No, they weren't," Jarratt replied softly. "I could never have married anyone else the way I feel about you. If you had been happy there, it would have been one thing. But you weren't, so I'm doing the one thing I know to do so that we can be together. Look, Cassandra, don't be upset. Even Dusty said I had no choice, and I figure he of all people should know. He loves a woman too, you know," he said softly as Cassandra's mouth flew open in astonishment. Dusty had said that Jarratt should sell!

"What about everybody back at the ranch?" Cassandra asked anxiously.

"Pete and Martha are going to retire, and B.C. is working on a neighboring ranch. Dusty's staying on. Enough about them," he said firmly. "What are you and I going to do?"

Cassandra's mind was whirling with options. Since Jarratt had already taken the irrevocable step and sold the ranch, she could not do the noble thing and talk him into keeping it. But where on earth would they live so that both of them would be happy? Jarratt may have sold the ranch in Pecos, but ranching was absolutely all he knew, and she knew that it would kill him to have to live in a city, especially one like Las Vegas.

"Jarratt, we need to talk," she began seriously, then lifted her hand reassuringly when Jarratt looked stricken. "No, I'm not changing my mind! Let's duck in here and get that coffee you wanted. I'm freezing," she said as she pointed to one of the hotel coffee shops.

The waitress had brought their coffee by the time Cassandra had returned from the ladies' room. She sipped the hot brew and stared into her cup thoughtfully. "Jarratt, I've done a lot of thinking since I've been back. I've

181

thought about those weeks in Texas. And, no, I couldn't have made it there. If we could have, I'd have gone back whether you wanted me or not. But if I had gone, we would have ended up just like your parents."

Jarratt nodded. "Then you think I did the right thing to sell?" he asked quietly.

"I guess so," Cassandra said sadly. "But it's always going to hurt me that you had to do it."

"I didn't have to," Jarratt reminded her softly. "I chose to. There's a big difference. It's no life to offer any woman, you or anybody else. Besides, I have to admit that sometimes I got lonely too. I was just used to it."

"You were lonely out there?" Cassandra exclaimed, astonished. "I thought you loved it."

"Parts of it I did," Jarratt acknowledged. "The horses, the peace . . ."

"The stars, the front porch swing," Cassandra continued softly. "The good parts. And there were some of those, Jarratt."

"You liked that?" Jarratt asked in astonishment. "I thought you hated it all."

"No, I didn't hate it all," Cassandra replied with tears shimmering in her eyes. "I liked that part of it. But, Jarratt, I simply have to have something to do with myself all day. Domesticity simply isn't enough for me."

"Fine," Jarratt reassured her, smiling broadly, taking a gulp of his coffee. "We stay here and I invest the money."

"God, no," Cassandra said disgustedly, sipping her coffee. "This is the last place I want to live. Anywhere but here, Jarratt. Please."

"You mean that," Jarratt replied incredulously. He laughed out loud. "You really mean that!"

"I'm glad you finally believe me," Cassandra replied dryly.

"That's a relief," Jarratt admitted. "So where? Do you want to buy a business in a city somewhere?"

Cassandra's eyes sparkled with excited anticipation. "Not really," she said.

Cassandra thought a moment, her shining eyes roving over her beloved rancher. "I'd like to buy a ranch," she said softly, sipping her cooling coffee.

"Cassandra, the comedians are supposed to be on the stage, not in the coffee shops," Jarratt said, groaning a little.

"No, I mean it, if it's possible," Cassandra replied earnestly. "Look, you're a rancher. That's all you know. I'm not about to take you away from that entirely." Her face became grim. "I've taken enough away from you already."

"Don't you ever feel like that!" Jarratt cautioned her.

"Sorry," Cassandra replied quickly.

"Anyway, what's the difference?" Jarratt continued. "I'm taking you away from the only thing you know."

"Not necessarily," Cassandra said slowly. "I'm just in the preliminary stages, but I've started a real estate course that I really like. I'll be certified in just a few months, and I could do that. So, I'm assuming you got a good price for the land?"

"Very good," Jarratt replied dryly.

"So we buy a ranch that isn't too far from a city or town," Cassandra said. "It would be expensive, I know, and it wouldn't be as big as your other one, but at least you would have your ranching and your cattle, and I'd be able to work in town. Is that possible, Jarratt? Could we do something like that?" She looked at him anxiously.

Jarratt's brows were knit in concentration. "I don't see why not," he said slowly. "If we found something down close to the coast near San Antonio or Corpus Christi, we wouldn't have to have as much land to raise the same

183

number of cattle. And if you didn't mind putting a few miles on the Firebird . . ."

"I don't mind a bit," Cassandra reassured Jarratt warmly.

Jarratt leaned over the table and kissed Cassandra on the nose. "I'll call my broker in the morning and tell him what we're looking for. By the time you're through with your courses, we'll have that ranch close to a city. Thanks, Cassandra," he said softly. "I would have missed it."

Cassandra nodded, happy tears in her eyes. "I know," she said softly as she swallowed the last of her coffee. She reached down into the cup with her fingers and picked up a thin band of sparkling diamonds.

"The next time I drink coffee with you, which should be tomorrow morning, I want you to have that on," Jarratt said softly. "Marry me tonight," he commanded her lovingly.

"In one of the chapels?" Cassandra asked doubtfully. "So soon? Don't you want to invite your friends?"

"Yes, yes, and no," Jarratt replied firmly. "In one of the chapels, tonight, and I want to wake up with my wife in my arms. All right?"

"All right," Cassandra replied softly, her heart overflowing with joy.

"Besides, you're already dressed for a wedding," Jarratt teased. He left money on the table, then as a thought occurred to him, he turned to Cassandra. "Do you know of a jeweler who's still open?"

"Why do we need a jeweler? Oh, for your ring." Cassandra nodded, and in a few minutes they had made their way to a hotel jeweler. Jarratt picked out a ring and while it was being sized, Cassandra wandered out into the casino, grateful she was leaving all this behind her. Jarratt joined her and they watched the games in progress for longer

184

than Cassandra really wanted to, then they collected Jarratt's ring and headed for the chapel.

The Justice of the Peace married them in a beautifully touching ceremony. In spite of the suddenness of the wedding, Cassandra felt every inch the bride, and as they left the chapel husband and wife, tears of joy shimmered in her eyes. Jarratt's ring sparkled on her finger and she held it out and admired it lovingly. Jarratt reached into his pocket, then took her hand and slipped another ring on her finger, on top of the wedding ring. Cassandra looked down and stared in wonder. It was her diamond heart, skillfully fashioned into an engagement ring. "What on earth? Jarratt Vandenburg, how did you manage that?"

"Cassandra Vandenburg, I bribed the jeweler," Jarratt grinned wickedly. "So that's not a good-bye present anymore. It's a good luck present for the gamble we just took."

"You know, Jarratt, I don't really think it's a gamble," Cassandra said softly, love shining in her eyes. "I think it's a sure bet."

"So do I," Jarratt murmured, bending to kiss her lips.

THE DARK HORSEMAN

Marianne Harvey

author of *The Proud Hunter*

Beautiful Donna Penroze had sworn to her dying father that she would save her sole legacy, the crumbling tin mines and the ancient, desolate estate *Trencobban*. But the mines were failing, and Donna had no one to turn to. No one except the mysterious Nicholas Trevarvas—rich, arrogant, commanding. Donna would do anything but surrender her pride, anything but admit her irresistible longing for *The Dark Horseman*.

A Dell Book $3.50

THE TAMING

Aleen Malcolm

Cameron—daring, impetuous girl/woman who has never known a life beyond the windswept wilds of the Scottish countryside.

Alex Sinclair—high-born and quick-tempered, finds more than passion in the heart of his headstrong ward Cameron.

Torn between her passion for freedom and her long-denied love for Alex, Cameron is thrust into the dazzling social whirl of 18th century Edinburgh and comes to know the fulfillment of deep and dauntless love. $3.50

A woman's place—the parlor, not the concert stage! But radiant Diana Ballantyne, pianist extraordinaire, had one year before she would bow to her father's wishes, return to England and marry. She had given her word, yet the moment she met the brilliant Maestro, Baron Lukas von Korda, her fate was sealed. He touched her soul with music, kissed her lips with fire, filled her with unnameable desire. One minute warm and passionate, the next aloof, he mystified her, tantalized her. She longed for artistic triumph, ached for surrender, her passions ignited by Vienna dreams.

$3.50

Vienna Dreams

by JANETTE RADCLIFFE

Seize The Dawn

by Vanessa Royall

For as long as she could remember, Elizabeth Rolfson knew that her destiny lay in America. She arrived in Chicago in 1885, the stunning heiress to a vast empire. As men of daring pressed westward, vying for the land, Elizabeth was swept into the savage struggle. Driven to learn the secret of her past, to find the one man who could still the restlessness of her heart, she would stand alone against the mighty to claim her proud birthright and grasp a dream of undying love. $3.50

At your local bookstore or use this handy coupon for ordering:

 DELL BOOKS
P.O. BOX 1000, PINE BROOK, N.J. 07058-1000

SEIZE THE DAWN   17788-X $3.50

B047D

Please send me the above title. I am enclosing $ _____ (please add 75c per copy to cover postage and handling). Send check or money order—no cash or C.O.D.'s. Please allow up to 8 weeks for shipment.

Mr./Mrs./Miss _____

Address _____

City _____ State/Zip _____